MORE NEWS TOMORROW

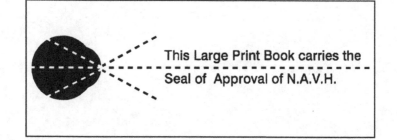

This Large Print Book carries the
Seal of Approval of N.A.V.H.

More News Tomorrow

WITHDRAWN

Susan Richards Shreve

THORNDIKE PRESS
A part of Gale, a Cengage Company

GALE
A Cengage Company

Farmington Hills, Mich • San Francisco • New York • Waterville, Maine
Meriden, Conn • Mason, Ohio • Chicago

Thorndike Press® Large Print Women's Fiction.
The text of this Large Print edition is unabridged.
Other aspects of the book may vary from the original edition.
Set in 16 pt. Plantin.

LIBRARY OF CONGRESS CIP DATA ON FILE.
CATALOGUING IN PUBLICATION FOR THIS BOOK
IS AVAILABLE FROM THE LIBRARY OF CONGRESS

ISBN-13: 978-1-4328-7000-3 (hardcover alk. paper)

Published in 2019 by arrangement with W. W. Norton, Inc.

Printed in Mexico
1 2 3 4 5 6 7 23 22 21 20 19

Isla Elizabeth
and
Timothy

May 7, 1945
Dear Georgianna,

I am unwell tonight. Some sense of foreboding that fate will intervene between us before I have an opportunity to tell you things as they were.

Just know that what you have been told is not the whole story. There will be more news tomorrow.

Your father
William Grove
(born Geringas, January 26, 1904
Vilnius, Lithuania)

A letter to Georgianna Grove found among the personal effects of William Grove following his death from pneumonia at the Illinois State prison, May 24, 1945

■ ■ ■ ■

HOME FOR THE INCURABLES

■ ■ ■ ■

December 17, 2007

GEORGIANNA

The letter from Roosevelt McCrary that upended Georgie's life came the morning of her seventieth birthday — written on Camp Minnie HaHa stationery and dated June 18, 2007. The handwriting sloped, the way Georgie's father's had been, the way children were taught to write script in the thirties — the paper smudged from handling. He must have written Georgie and then reread the letter again and again for months before he decided to mail it.

Dear Georgianna,
　You may not remember me. I was eleven and you were four and your mother was thirty-three and your father was thirty-seven when I last saw you and now I am seventy-seven and you must be seventy this year and I wish you a very Happy Birthday. If you are receiving this letter and have any interest in

hearing from me, here I am. I have lived as a groundskeeper and general carpenter at your father's camp since I was twenty-four, thirteen years after your mother died. In time I became a part owner and now live at the camp in retirement but still keep the grounds, repair the occasional chair or cabin window.

There were nine people on the canoe trip in 1941 and all of them are dead but you and me. I remember the morning your mother was discovered just above the sign for Missing Lake. Did you know that? Missing Lake, Wisconsin, a two-hour trip upriver by canoe to Minnie HaHa. For days it had been raining and that morning the sky opened and the yellow sun was rising in the east and I thought to myself, Finally the sun.

And then James Willow, the head counselor, and a former student of your father's from Chicago, traveling in the third and last boat, discovered your mother on the ground at the edge of the pine forest.

I am so sorry.
Yours truly,
Roosevelt McCrary

PS. James Willow died in 1943 as a fighter pilot in WWII. I got your address from information. I hope I'm not intruding.

When the mailman arrived, Georgie was in the kitchen taking down the dishes from the cupboard to set the table for the birthday party that she was giving herself that evening.

A rack of lamb marinating in mint and garlic on the counter, sweet parsnips to be pureed on the stove, bubbling in milk, French green beans, roasted carrots. The color of things mattered to Georgie, cooking her way through the cookbooks she read at night before she went to sleep. Rosie had made a chocolate cassis cake with raspberries for dessert.

Autumn sunlight spilled across the open porch, a light breeze like summer — not rare for Washington in mid-December, but the heat of the day was unusual.

She waved to the mailman through the bank of windows that framed the front door, and he handed her the large stack of mail, catalogues, throwaway advertisements, bills.

"And this," he said giving her the handwritten brown envelope, ripped on the edges, something yellow spilled across the address so the destination was barely visible, the stamp half gone. "It must have had a helluva trip."

A letter — just the fact of it — was significant.

An actual letter out of nowhere into this brilliant morning in northwest Washington, D.C.

She sat down on the top step of the porch and opened the envelope.

News from Camp Minnie HaHa. Her first home, the home to which she had arrived as an infant traveling the Bone River with her parents by canoe.

She read the letter slowly, read it twice and didn't realize that the breath had gone out of her until she stood, leaning for balance, against a pillar on the front porch. Lightheaded, she walked back in the house, passing the living room, where her grandson, Thomas, who had just turned thirteen, was lying on his side in front of the fireplace, reading.

A Monday and Thomas had not gone to school again.

"Any interesting mail for me?" he called.

"Only one and it's for me," she replied.

"For your birthday," Thomas said without looking up from his book.

"More interesting than that."

14

She would tell Thomas about the letter. Sometime, not today. He knew about her mother's murder at a campsite on the Bone River, and somehow it delighted him to hear her tell about it as if the value of Thomas' own life were enhanced by his genetic proximity to such a story.

Georgie folded the letter, put it in the envelope and walked up the back staircase to her room, slipping it in her underwear drawer beneath a small stack of camisoles and worn bras.

She needed new underwear. She had noticed that hers had gotten thin and gray with washing, holes in the crotch of her panties. Maybe she'd buy those slips of colorful lace bikinis that Rosie wore.

Seventy, but no reason to settle into a life without intimacy — in fact she'd recently read in one of the magazines at the dentist's that for older women intimacy was fundamental to health and spirit. She didn't need a magazine for that news.

She stood at her dresser checking herself in the long mirror. She had a slender, striking face, high cheekbones, olive skin, large dark eyes — intimations still of the young woman she had been.

How many months — actually years —

15

had it been? She'd been sixty-five when Edward Connell, with whom she'd occasionally been sleeping, moved with his wife back to Nebraska. Too far to continue a relationship, and Georgie was not sufficiently urgent for Edward to meet, say, in New York or Chicago.

Besides, things happened. Nicolas' daughter Oona was born; Rosie's husband Richard got sick and died. In the months after Richard's death, Thomas, their son, developed a speech pattern that prevented him from completing a sentence, so his conversations, except in the safety of home, became a series of beginnings without ends. And just this past summer, Georgie's youngest child Venus went into a facility for alcohol abuse and came back to the Home for the Incurables to live One Day at a Time.

Georgie wanted a love affair. Someone younger perhaps who could expand inside her without all the trouble it had taken Edward. Or even someone older who would lie beside her, their bodies curled together in the large four-poster bed on the second floor of the Home for the Incurables, and talk her into the night. Someone whose voice was the sound she heard as she fell asleep.

Since Charley really, she had never wanted

16

a man living in her house with his big shoes needing polishing and his briefcase and papers and newspapers and undershorts and the television on all the time. Just a visitor who came and went at *her* discretion and kept his things — his clothes and books and loose change and cash receipts — elsewhere.

Which had nothing to do with Charley, whom she would love for the rest of her life.

Something about Roosevelt thinking of her after so many years filled her with happiness. Or maybe he had often thought of her but never had the courage to write before.

Happy Birthday, he had written. *I wish you a very happy birthday.*

Like a love letter.

When Thomas came up the back stairs, Georgie was checking the gray circles hanging in half moons under her eyes, thinking what could be done to get rid of them. She turned from the mirror to find him leaning against the entrance to her bedroom

"I didn't even hear you on the stairs," she said.

"I didn't want you to hear me."

Thomas was tall and very thin. Quite beautiful, Georgie thought — blond curls and full lips, high color — a wariness about him, pale blue eyes, turned inward.

"Maybe Thomas is *so* brilliant he doesn't need to go to school," Nicolas, the eldest of her children, had said, annoyed at Georgie's preference for Thomas over *his* son, Jesse. "Or he could be on the spectrum, which is gaining in national popularity."

His father had been a brilliant scientist, but who knew about Thomas. What he did was *read* all the time, recently *Middlemarch* — was there a child in *Middlemarch*? Georgie had asked him — and the comedies of Shakespeare. *The tragedies are too sad for a boy my age,* he said. *The Odyssey.*

In place of schoolwork, or hanging out after school with friends, or athletics on the weekends despite being very good at baseball — he was writing a series of comic novels about an invisible boy with unpredictable powers, called *The Boy.*

"The Boy takes up space," Thomas explained to Georgie. "You just can't see him."

"You can touch him?"

"You can't exactly touch him, but you're blocked if you try to move into the space his body occupies."

Thomas braced against the wall at the top of the stairs.

"When are you coming back downstairs?"

18

She was standing at her open closet door considering what she would wear for her birthday.

"In just a minute."

"I came up to ask you something about William Grove."

"I don't know much about my father," she said, taking her black silk pants out of the closet and hanging them on the doorknob. "I was four years old the last time I saw him and he died when I was eight."

"I think I'm going to write him into my novel as a character — probably the invisible boy's grandfather. He'll be an interesting character but dead, and the boy is beginning to understand that he has the power to bring him back to life."

She closed her closet door, pulled up the covers on the unmade bed, put her nightshirt under the pillow.

"You need to go to school more often, Thomas," she said.

Georgie had told Thomas about William Grove when his own father had died. She was at the apartment in Chicago helping Rosie after the funeral, sitting one morning at the bottom of Rosie and Richard's bed — Thomas at the window, his head pressed against the glass, looking out at summer over the lake.

"*I was four* when my mother was killed . . . ," she began, ". . . and I knew too little about the world to be heartbroken."

Thomas turned away from the window.

"Do you want me to continue?"

He nodded.

"Tell me everything."

"For chrissake, Georgie . . ." Nicolas had said later. "Maybe you could have waited a couple of years to tell him about your father. Or at least let his *mother,* Rosie, tell him."

"Sometimes you have the right moment," Georgie said.

"Or the absolute wrong moment," Nicolas said.

But over time the unfinished story of William Grove was sufficient to sustain Thomas' imagination.

Georgie turned off the overhead light, heading to the kitchen, and Thomas followed down the winding back stairs, slithering along the curving steps, snakelike, barely aware of his body and how he moved, disengaged from his physical self, half in another world.

"Do you ever *wonder* what really happened to your mother?" he asked.

"Wonder?" Georgie took the carrots out of the fridge.

"I wonder about it all the time."

"I don't have any context for what happened at Missing Lake except to know who was on that trip, since their names were listed in the June 21, 1941, issue of the *Chicago Tribune*."

"You showed me that story in the *Tribune*."

"That's all I really know."

"You never asked your grandparents?"

She shook her head.

"I was only four when my mother was killed, and the night after her body was discovered, I went to Ann Arbor, Michigan, to live with them."

"I would have had a ton of questions."

"They wouldn't have answered your questions. My grandparents were midwestern Protestants and never talked. It was as if my mother — my *beautiful mother,* as they referred to her — vanished without a trace and my father's only defining character was Jew."

"My father was also a Jew," Thomas said.

"And a scientist and very smart and handsome and a sweetheart."

Georgie got out a chopping board and took a long blade knife from the drawer.

21

"I have no information about my father." She leaned against the kitchen counter. "My mother must have been strangled sometime in the night. In the morning, my father was taken away by the police. I watched him get in the police boat, but that is all I remember."

Thomas slid into a kitchen chair, knocking the salt off the table and then the yellow tulips wrapped in brown paper and stuck in a glass of water.

"Thomas!"

He leaned over to pick up the tulips.

"I mean William Grove went to jail and he didn't have to go to jail, right?" Thomas asked, wiping up the water on the floor. "He could have said, *Oh my god, I haven't a clue what happened,* and probably the police would have believed him because after all your mother was his wife."

"The salt, Thomas. Could you sweep it up?"

He got the broom and swept up the salt, mopped the water, slipped back in the chair.

"Do you forgive him?"

"I don't want to talk about this. Not on my birthday while I'm cooking, which is something I love to do, and sitting with you, something I also love to do."

■ ■ ■ ■

Georgie was still lightheaded from the letter, her hands numb as she scraped the carrots, the beating of her heart off center as if the heart itself had moved to the right in the middle of her chest.

"How about instead we discuss the word *forgive,* which I looked up in the Oxford."

Thomas hopped onto a wooden kitchen chair with a rush seat, crouched froglike as he often did, wrapping his arms around his knees.

"*Forgive* has a lot of meanings, but the one I am thinking about is '*forgive* means to give up anger,' and I cannot give up anger about the fact that some of the kids at Alice Deal Junior High School don't want to be around me because my father died."

"Why is that?"

"They think they can catch my father's death as if it's a germ and I'm contagious."

"Is that why you don't want to go to school?"

"Maybe it is," he said.

Georgie gathered the carrots and washed them under the tap, dried them, set them on the cutting board to slice.

"People can be afraid of bad news," she

said. "But you should ignore the ones who think that death is catching. Because it isn't."

"It kind of is," Thomas said, rocking back and forth on his haunches, testing the old wooden chair for stability. "What about you and your father?"

"If I needed to forgive my father, I would have to believe he was guilty," Georgie said. "I don't believe he was."

"I guess we'll never know."

"Maybe that's true."

Georgie was chopping the carrots in crayon-size strips, sprinkling salt, grinding pepper, lining them side by side in a broiler pan to roast.

"Or maybe we will," she added, thinking as she spoke — quite without considering what she was saying — that she *would* tell Thomas about the letter from Roosevelt McCrary *now* in the kitchen making dinner for her seventieth birthday party.

Thomas would have a plan of action. He always did.

So she told him.

Because it was her birthday and she was seventy and the two of them were alone in the Home for the Incurables — no one else to tell except Georgie's own children who were more ashamed of the story of her

24

father than interested in it.

Only Thomas had taken on the night of June 17, 1941, when Josephine Grove was strangled, as a story of great and extraordinary importance to him and to his whole family and likely to the world.

Which it had been. Which it was, still, at the core of Georgie's life.

"There is only one person still alive who was at the campsite on the Bone River when my mother was murdered," Georgie said, her low-pitched voice cracking as it sometimes did. "His name is Roosevelt McCrary and the letter that came today for me is from him."

"Did you know about him?" Thomas asks.

"I knew there was one other child at the campsite, but he was never identified by name in the newspaper stories because he was a child."

"This is excellent news!" Thomas said. "Are you telling everybody at your party tonight?'

"I don't know," Georgie said, reaching into the back of the fridge where she'd hidden the butter from the tenants. "I wasn't going to tell *you* and then I did."

Thomas was standing at the open fridge examining the shelves of food.

"I wish Mr. Egland didn't cook everything with garlic so the fridge smells like Mr. Egland instead of food," he said.

"I don't like it either."

"Sometimes I also wish you didn't have so many strangers around, sleeping in your beds, eating at your kitchen table and stuff."

Georgie sliced the butter into neat squares.

"I have strangers around intentionally," she said. "I wanted a home for my children after Charley died and this is how I made one. To make a home, you need a tribe."

"When I need someone, I make her up," Thomas said. "That's how I happen to have Lucy Elliott, who is my height with long red hair and she's hanging out in my new Invisible Boy book. Crazy about me."

He took an apple and shut the refrigerator door.

"Garlic apple," he said leaving, the kitchen door swinging on its hinges.

"Okay if I make a fire?"

"It's too warm for a fire."

But Thomas was making one anyway. Georgie could hear him carrying in the wood from the front porch, a clatter from the dining room already set for dinner . . . singing,

"Let me call you sweetheart, I'm in love with

you / Let me hear you whisper that you love me too."

Always the old romantic songs were the ones he loved. His voice soprano slipping toward tenor.

Then he was back in the kitchen, loose bark from the logs dropping from his clothes onto the kitchen floor.

"I was just wondering — have you ever been back to Camp Minnie HaHa?" he asked, brushing off his hands in the sink.

"Never," Georgie said.

"How come?"

"There was no reason to go back. No one was there who might have known me."

She wiped her wet hands on her trousers.

"Then why don't you go to meet Roosevelt *now*?" Thomas asked, sitting on the end of the kitchen table swinging his legs. "I can't believe that wasn't the first thing you wanted to do when you got his letter."

"I haven't thought of *doing* something about the letter," she said, taking the wineglasses down from the cupboard. "Except to write him back."

But that was not exactly true.

Already Georgie was imagining her first meeting with Roosevelt. He'd be standing on the bank of the river at Camp Minnie

HaHa in jeans and a work shirt, maybe a baseball cap, waiting for her to arrive by canoe. She had no actual memory of him, only that there was another child besides her in the group camping at Missing Lake. Something she knew from the newspaper accounts her grandmother had saved for her to read when she was old enough.

In the article printed in the June 21, 1941, *Chicago Tribune,* Roosevelt's mother was listed as Clementine McCrary, age thirty-three, but Roosevelt was given no identity by name.

"Let's go this summer right after school's out in June," Thomas said.

Georgie was distracted. Standing at the sink, her back to Thomas, she nearly chopped off the tip of her index finger slicing shallots with a dull knife — now the bloody finger wrapped in a paper towel leaking in the drain, her thoughts careening, scrambling her brain.

What might Roosevelt tell her when they meet? What had he seen at the campsite? He must remember her father since he was already eleven that summer. At eleven, a boy would remember a murder.

Does he remember Georgie? Does he think about her because of the tragedy? Has he been wondering for years what became of her?

"We can rent canoes," Thomas was saying. "We'll stop at the exact same place where your mother was murdered. Sort of like the thing you do with maps in Botswana, finding stuff, studying ancient tribes imagining what might have happened thousands of years ago. What do you think?"

"I think this, Thomas," Georgie said. "Tonight, I'm giving myself a birthday party and hoping not to overcook the lamb."

By late afternoon, Georgie had sat down on the couch in the kitchen with the dissertation of one of her graduate students in cultural anthropology. Thomas upstairs in his bedroom was writing "William Grove into my book," as he told her. The dining room table was set with Georgie's grandmother's silver, a deep blue and wine woven cloth she'd brought home that summer from Botswana, a vase of yellow tulips spilling over the rim, votives scattering the dining room table with light, wood banked in the fireplace, CDs of early Beatles and Frank Sinatra waiting in the sound system.

She had even made place cards, although there were only seven of them, in a tight group at the end of the long refectory table.

Georgie's blood. All that remained:

Nicolas — his wife Olivia would be absent, playing Desdemona in *Othello* at the Folger Theatre. Jesse and Oona, their children. Rosie, her older daughter. Thomas. And Venus, the child Charley had left behind.

But she was not in a humor to read student work. She stuffed the dissertation back in her book bag, took a piece of paper from the drawer — not the formal gray stationery with *Georgianna Grove* in white lettering at the top; nor the George Washington University office stationery with "Dr. Georgianna Grove, Professor of Cultural Anthropology," on the left.

But plain recycled computer paper.

Sitting at the kitchen table, she ran her sweatered arm across the top of the table to clean the residue from cooking and took a pen out of her back pocket.

It must have taken Roosevelt days to write that letter. Weeks to send it.

"You are not intruding, Roosevelt McCrary," she wrote, her eyes filling with unexpected tears. *"I have been waiting for sixty-six years to receive this and now it has come and I thank you from the bottom of my heart."*

At her grandparents' house in Ann Arbor, Georgie's bedroom was under the eaves on the third floor. A small room painted white with a circle of tiny windows like portholes from which she could peer at the garden where her grandmother was weeding or clipping or planting and Georgie could not be seen. There she spent hours playing *family* with paper dolls who lived their organized lives in shoe boxes lined up under her bed. Twenty families in twenty shoe boxes with mothers and fathers and brothers and sisters and cousins and aunts and uncles spread out the afternoons of winter all over the carpet. Georgie took on the role of village doctor moving from shoe box to shoe box caring for the sick members of her imagined paper community.

She had had in mind becoming a physician, but when she entered the University of Michigan as a premed student in 1955, it was a class in introductory cultural anthropology, the study of human life in groups, rather than the chemistry of the body, that captured her attention.

In graduate school, the subject of her dissertation was home.

HOME: Among the Baos Tribe in Botswana — the title of her first book published for an audience of ordinary readers as well as for academics, a book about primitive communities or villages or tribes — how a life

31

led in common with others, related or unrelated, came into being, how the human animal and animals in general are interdependent, creating by association a common narrative, willing to sacrifice individual needs in order to belong to a larger whole. Empathetic by nature.

She was a scholar, although she thought of herself, more simply, as a storyteller, imagining the lives that might have been lived from bits of evidence she collected and put in order.

Home. Just the sound of it could make her weep. The hush, the long *o,* the hum of the letter *m.*

Charley MacDowell had died in a mine blast at the Battle of Ong Thanh, October 17, 1967, three months after he had arrived on the front as a volunteer physician in Vietnam. He was thirty-one. Nicolas was four, Rosie was two and Georgie, four months pregnant with Venus, was twenty-nine.

The children were with her that morning — 9:15, a Tuesday in October — when the officers arrived at her house in Foggy Bottom with the news.

She listened tearless to the one officer say what had happened, how the United States government and President Johnson were

32

grateful for Dr. MacDowell's service to his country, and because she did not move from the door or ask them to come in and speak to her in the safety of her own home, they nodded, a moment of silence, bowed and left.

Nothing in her fractured life had allowed her to believe that Charley would return alive from Vietnam.

An afternoon, weeks later, early December, she walked miles from her house in Foggy Bottom, just a walk to slough off the accumulating sadness, skipping her tutorials at George Washington University, walking north toward Maryland, in the direction of Friends School, where she'd put Nicolas when his father was killed.

A Quaker school, a choice made in quiet protest against the violence of war.

It was the first time she had talked to Charley since he died, something she did even now and especially when she was walking.

"I must tell you, Charley," she began quietly, the way she always began their conversations, turning her head slightly to the right. Things she felt a need to tell him, to hear herself tell him, as if he were beside her. Listening.

But Charley was dead.

"It's been a terrible pregnancy. I've been to the hospital twice for bleeding, and I cry all night, my door shut so the children won't hear me. I need for them to think *I'm fine. Just fine.* A dead father can happen to children and maybe they'll see you later. Maybe at Christmas. But I don't say that of course since they won't see you at Christmas. Or ever, for that matter. Although you should know you left one child behind with me."

It *worked* talking to Charley like that.

In the short term, at least, she was in the presence of his company.

That afternoon at Upton Street, just off Wisconsin Avenue and a block short of Friends School, she'd come upon a large square building with a porch, maybe a private home, maybe a school, dark brick, overgrown with shrubbery in the front, a FOR SALE sign planted in the yard.

On the brass plate over the front door THE HOME FOR THE INCURABLES was embossed.

Home for the Incurables.

Something in the name appealed to her. *Incurables?*

Had it been a place for people who were sick and would never get well and they never did get well and now they were gone?

34

Or is everyone in some way an incurable, and if one were to gather people together who did not belong to one another, wouldn't that be an act of hope?

The door was unlocked and Georgie went inside, through the vestibule, into the enormous living room with a walk-in fireplace, the dining room large enough for a small boarding school, up the back stairs to the second floor and the third. Ten bedrooms in all.

There was no evidence of what the house had been and who had lived there except in the name. Nothing except the terrible stench of dead raccoons trapped in the vestibule.

"I probably wouldn't buy a place of death like this," she told the real estate agent that day, "except I'm having a baby."

Even before the agent left that first afternoon, the Home for the Incurables was becoming a place for a family in process, her own family and maybe the families of others, even strangers off the street who would become friends, like family, students from the university, her own teaching assistants.

Here in this doomed house, she could create a community of strangers, open up the windows, paint the walls in the colors of the earth absorbing the sun, fill the kitchen shelves, the large wall space lined with bookcases, children's art spread across the rooms, maybe a carousel horse in the living room. And cats.

That night she lay in her four-poster bed and filled the rooms of the Home for the Incurables the way she used to do with paper dolls in her grandmother's attic.

There'd be a long table in the dining room, and the guests — she would think of them as guests — would join her at the table, take Rosie onto their laps and read to her, play games of Scrabble with Nicolas. Adopted aunts and uncles, children who would take on the role of the cousins Georgie could not provide.

Her grandmother's family was too small. Only one child, Georgie's mother, dead at thirty-three. And Georgie. No information about her father. He had brothers, but were they still alive? Were there cousins her age? Did everyone leave Lithuania before Hitler took over?

Georgie has been in search of her father all of her remembered life.

Since her parents disappeared at Missing Lake, gone in the morning when she woke up and peered out of the tent at a tornado of confusion, her father in a police boat on the river, Georgie whisked to Ann Arbor to live with her grandparents.

It was not until she was eight, and not because she was told, that she began to understand her parents would not be returning to pick her up. That her mother was dead and finally her father was dead.

The morning after she saw the house on Upton Street, Georgie called the real estate agent with an offer.

"You're quite sure you want this house, Dr. Grove?" the agent asked. "It's a bit of a dump."

"Yes it is," she agreed. "But I have a plan for it."

THE HOME FOR THE INCURABLES, the brass plate still over the door, was where Georgie had lived for forty-one years and raised her children and taken in strangers, eighty-nine strangers since 1968 not counting graduate students. And cats.

Rosie came home from her studio in Adams Morgan just after six. She was in the living room standing next to the fireplace in her coat when Georgie came downstairs.

She and Thomas were having an argument about school, rare for Rosie, who did not like trouble.

"I'll go tomorrow, Mama," Georgie overheard Thomas say as she walked by the living room and stopped to listen. "but I don't find school useful to me now."

There was a pause — his voice rose and cracked when he spoke.

"You probably know that our English assignment for seventh grade is to write a memoir of our lives so far — but why would I want to write a memoir when what I would rather do is write about forgetting."

"Well . . ." Rosie began but her voice trailed off and she followed Georgie to the kitchen, opened a pot on the stove with the parsnips and dipped her finger in, licking it.

"Yum. Potatoes?"

"Parsnips," Georgie said.

"Even better," she said. "I suppose it *is* strange to have thirteen-year-olds writing a memoir when nothing has happened to them."

"Childhood has happened to them," Georgie said. "Certainly to Thomas."

Rosie made a cup of tea and sat down at the kitchen table, her feet up on a chair, oddly quiet, looking just past Georgie at the oven as if something there had captured her attention.

"*You* could have written a memoir at

thirteen," Rosie said.

Georgie was wary of a serious conversation with Rosie just now — her birthday, a plan for the evening, her emotions too close to the surface to trust.

Rosie rested her chin in her hand.

"You never talk about your father as a person. I've noticed that. Not the way you told us about our father and what we had missed not knowing him."

"I didn't know my father as a person." She shook her head. "I don't know where to find him."

"But that's what you do," Rosie said. "You find things."

She got up and opened the door to the fridge, taking out the chocolate cassis cake she had made for Georgie's birthday, sniffing the top of it.

"Garlic?" Georgie asked.

"Chocolate," Rosie said, leaving the cake on the counter, sitting across from Georgie at the kitchen table.

"Do you want to hear about my day?"

Usually, Georgie listened to Rosie when she came home from her studio, even happy to be included in her work, but this evening she felt the slightest irritation.

"I am doing a kitchen — a twelve-by-eighteen canvas." Rosie tilted her chair back. "You're sure you don't mind this talk about my painting on your birthday?"

"You know I don't."

Every evening when Rosie came home from Adams Morgan, she talked about her day. Show-and-tell, as if she were a schoolgirl. And there *was* something girlish about her — even at forty-two. Delight in what she saw and painted. Lately, she had been painting rooms of domesticity vacant of people, colors melting across the canvas. Interiors with windows looking out on an eerie light with thin lines the color of vermilion.

"I'm painting these tomatoes on a farm table in an old-fashioned kitchen — green, sort of parrot green tomatoes — which may be the problem," Rosie was saying. "They're half-sliced on a mustard yellow plate, and I'm trying to capture the sense that the *someone* cutting the tomatoes has suddenly been called away — by an emergency, not just to pee — so it isn't a still life I'm doing. But the person who should be in the painting has left, and though the colors are warm, there is something menacing about the scene. You know what I mean?"

"I do," Georgie said, brushing a sweet butter glaze on the carrots ready to roast.

But she didn't understand. Irritated by

40

the absence of people in Rosie's paintings
— not a shadow of a person.

Georgie took it personally.

"And then I had a late lunch with Max."

You always have lunch with Max went
through Georgie's mind and stopped there.

Max Rider had the studio next to Rosie's
and Georgie did not like him. Nor did she
think it was good for Thomas that his
mother had the facsimile of a boyfriend so
soon after Richard's death.

Two years! Rosie would say. *I'm not like
you. Two years is an eternity.*

Georgie poured the parsnips and milk into
the mixer.

"Is Venus going to be home on time?" Rosie asked.

"She's upstairs in her room dressing for
tonight. She had her hair cut."

"Short?"

"She looks exactly like Nicolas without a
beard."

"You should know she's planning a Tarot
reading for tonight," Rosie said.

"I was hoping she would."

"I was hoping *not,*" Rosie said. "And be
honest, Georgie. You don't want a reading
for your seventieth birthday. It's bound to
be grim."

Venus read Tarot cards for a living and

was known in the city for her work, although it did not pay a living wage.

A funny girl, Georgie thought about Venus. Odd and disarming. Tall, lanky like Charley and awkward, with an appealing freckled face.

Her birth certificate read Madeleine, but by the time she was in seventh grade, she had changed it to Venus.

"Because of Mary Madeleine in the Bible," she had told Georgie.

"Magdalene," Georgie said.

"She was a prostitute. I love that, don't you? A prostitute right there in the middle of the New Testament."

Venus' room at the Home for the Incurables was on the top floor in the back of the house, a cozy room with its own bath and sitting room. But most nights unless she was between relationships she spent away.

"I'm kind of a sex addict, Georgie," Venus had said. "I can't seem to help it."

"Oona's here!" Thomas called from the vestibule. "And Jesse."

"And Uncle Nicolas," Nicolas called.

Nicolas had come alone — straight from the airport on a regular domestic flight from Detroit, where Obama was speaking. He'd left his work with the Obama Press Corps

42

traveling in the first leg of his campaign for president in order to arrive in time for Georgie's birthday, stopping at home to pick up Oona and Jesse.

"Georgie my singular mother." Nicolas kissed the top of her head. "Happy birthday. What news today? Thomas tells me something is up."

"Did he tell you what it was?"

"Thomas? Are you kidding? And miss the opportunity for a dramatic revelation? So you have news?"

"I do," Georgie said.

Upstairs she had dressed for the evening. A fitted gray-lavender top, tight at the waist with an Asian-style stiff collar and black trousers. She had the figure for it — a long neck, long-waisted, flat stomach. Hips. She still wore deep red lipstick and blush on her high cheekbones, her hair swept up in combs.

Just before she went downstairs, she slipped Roosevelt's letter from the folds of a black camisole and tucked it into the waist of her trousers.

Small — the group assembled on the night of December 17 at the long refectory table in the dining room.

43

Nicolas and Rosie and Venus, Nicolas with Oona, who was four, and Jesse, a sullen, ill-tempered fifteen. Rosie and Thomas. Venus, solo, although she had a new boyfriend, but as she told her family, she had only spent the night with him once.

Not good enough, she said about her overnight. Quick to come to decisions.

Kubla, Thomas' curly-coated retriever puppy was under the table chewing a snow boot belonging to Rosie. The cats sleeping around the living room, as if they had been acquired for decoration and obliged.

The other permanent residents of the Home — eight of them that December — were upstairs in their rooms or out to dinner or spending the evening with friends. By request, they were not to use the kitchen.

"I do have news," Georgie said when they sat down at the table.

"Shall I say grace?" Nicolas asked, as if grace before dinner were a part of family ritual.

"I thought grace was about God," Thomas said. "Like the grace of God that passeth all understanding."

"Grace is a variable," Georgie said.

"Whatever," Jesse said, a word he'd recently added to his small vocabulary, which included *brain dead* and *fuck.*

Georgie took Roosevelt's letter out of the waistband of her trousers, flattening it with the palm of her hand. She reached over and pulled the lit candelabra to her place at the table so she could see to read.

"Here comes trouble," Nicolas said.

"This is a letter I received today," she began, ignoring Nicolas, "written on Camp Minnie HaHa stationery from a man called Roosevelt McCrary who was on the trip when my mother was killed."

"This is not boding well," Nicolas said.

"Let her read it, Nicolas," Rosie said. "It's her birthday."

"Don't talk about Georgie in the third person," Venus said. "She's sitting right here in front of us about to read a letter of great importance. I can see her. *Voilà!*"

"I don't know what's coming in that letter, Georgie," Nicolas said, "but I'm amazed — we are all amazed except maybe Thomas — at how easily you float between the real world and an imagined one when after all you're a scientist."

"This news *is* the real world," Georgie said, "and I have decided to make tonight a celebration of Roosevelt's arrival in my life. That's all."

"His arrival?" Nicolas asked. "Apparently he has always been in your life but you failed to tell us."

"I didn't *know*. I read about him in the newspaper reports of what happened when my mother was killed, but I've never heard from anyone who was on the trip, so Roosevelt's letter after so many years, nearly my lifetime, was a complete surprise."

Nicolas poured himself another glass of wine.

He was as tall as Charley had been, dark-haired and wiry, with an edge that put his family slightly on guard. An occasional temper.

"Why should the appearance of Roosevelt be good news?" he asked.

"I didn't say it's good news or bad," Georgie said. "It's news that makes me very happy. That's all."

"It's very good news and it makes me happy too," Thomas said. "Finally we'll get to know for real whether Georgie's father killed his wife on June 17, 1941. Or not."

Her children seldom talked about Georgie's past. Not her mother's murder, nor her father's confession, except among themselves and that occasionally since it had been *their* father's death in Vietnam that dominated their childhoods.

But if the subject of the murder came up,

46

Georgie would say — known to dramatize her life as if the one she *had* lived needed extra effort — that her father was innocent and confessed to the murder to protect someone else.

"It's complicated news, Thomas," Nicolas said. "More than you can possibly understand. We're living in present time and the past, at least in this family, is very disturbing."

"How come disturbing?" Thomas asked.

"Come off it, Thomas," Nicolas said. "In an ordinary family, it would be *disturbing* to know that your grandfather had killed his wife."

"It may be that Roosevelt has something on his mind to tell us," Georgie said. "We may get news."

"I'm sure he does have something on his mind." Nicolas got up from the table to attend the fire.

"He probably needs money," Venus said.

"It's nothing about money," Georgie said. "Roosevelt McCrary was eleven years old and happened to be at Missing Lake when everything exploded. My father had hired him to work at the camp that summer. Of course, he probably does know *something.*"

Venus got up from the table, heading to her room.

"I'm going to read your cards tonight, Georgie," Venus said. "I'll do it right now, if you'd like."

"She wouldn't like it now, Venus," Nicolas said. "We're about to eat and drink. A lot — especially a lot of drink."

"Be a little sensitive, Nicolas," Rosie said. "Georgie's right. Roosevelt might very well know something."

"Something, I'm sure," Nicolas said. "But it may be something we'd rather not know ourselves."

"Who exactly are we?" Venus asked.

"We are the *originals*. Seven of us sitting at this table related by *blood,*" Georgie said. "When we go to Camp Minnie HaHa in June to meet Roosevelt, we'll have a chance to find out what he knows."

"We?" Nicolas asked.

"That's my birthday present to myself," Georgie said. "I'm taking all of you with me next summer to Camp Minnie HaHa to meet Roosevelt."

"That will not include me," Nicolas said.

"It *will* include you, Nicolas," Georgie said cheerfully. "I have already written to Roosevelt that we're coming and reserved the canoes."

■ ■ ■ ■

THE BONE RIVER

■ ■ ■ ■

June 16, 2008

They arrived at five at Blake's Lodge and Outfitters in Riverton, Wisconsin. The town of Riverton was no more than a gas station, a convenience store and Blake's located on the edge of the Bone River, roaring this early evening as if a storm were charging up from the riverbed. The six of them had left from Washington Reagan, meeting Nicolas at Chicago O'Hare and driving north in a large rental van that seated seven. Georgie's plan, arranged to accommodate Nicolas' schedule on the campaign with Obama, was to be gone two days and three nights, the first night in the lodge in Riverton. One day on the river to Missing Lake, where they would spend the night. A short day to Minnie HaHa for the second night. Late the following morning, a worker from the Outfitters would drive their rental van up to Minnie HaHa to pick up the family. A motorboat from the Outfitters would pick up the three canoes at the dock of the camp and take them back to Riverton. Georgie's family would drive on to Chicago in the rental van to board their flight to Washington and Nicolas's to meet the Obama team in Michigan. Hillary Clinton had withdrawn from the presidential race in early June and it was possible that Obama, running against John McCain, would be the next president of the United States, which made it all the more difficult for Nicolas to be away from the campaign.

When he met his family in Chicago, he was at a low boil.

The owner of the outfitters, Mr. Blake, had told Georgie there was no reason to make such complicated arrangements with canoes and a pickup van.

"I understand it was hard to get to the camp in 1941, Ms. Grove, but it's 2008 and we've got roads and you could be up there in a van and back in Chicago in a day and a half and never have to get in a canoe."

"That's not the point," Georgie said. "This is a canoe trip and I'm happy to pay whatever extra costs for you to pick up the canoes and us."

"Suit yourself," he said. "We're glad to have you." There was a pause. "You're familiar with canoes on rivers, I assume."

"Rivers, lakes. I haven't been in a canoe for a long time, but I can surely paddle," Georgie said.

"There's a difference between canoeing on a lake and canoeing on a river."

"Yes, of course," Georgie said.

"Current," Mr. Blake said. "Bring warm clothes. June is cold."

And that was that.

"Georgie?" Nicolas asked, leaving the lodge after they had made the arrangements with Mr. Blake, paid the rest of the bill, gotten their room keys for the night. "Did you check out the current on the river?"

"Not yet," she said. "It's a calm evening."

Nicolas walked with Georgie to the bank — dusk, a beautiful crisp summer night, the moon clear and slender.

"What do you think?" Nicolas asked.

"About the current?"

"Exactly," he said. "Listen."

"I can *see* it."

"We're not exactly a boating family."

"Well, maybe not, but you went to camp and so did Venus and Jesse. Rosie says Thomas is excellent on the water." She inched down the bank. "I know how to canoe. I mean I've been out in a canoe on the Potomac River."

"Once?"

"Or twice."

"At least we need to ask Mr. Blake some questions about this river. I know nothing about rivers and I think our family would justifiably be considered novices."

"We'll take life preservers."

"Well, of course. But look at the water. Even in a life preserver . . ."

"I understand, Nicolas. I know what you're saying and I did take danger into account when I was planning this trip." She spoke with a calm exasperation that had developed over years of teaching.

But in actual fact, Georgie had taken very little into account.

Canoes on a river, a narrow river in northern Wisconsin with four adults. Easy to swim to the bank if a canoe capsized. Or so it appeared. Certainly they wouldn't put in if there were a storm. They'd take every precaution. But she actually had not given *danger* any thought. She believed herself capable of accommodating circumstance. An orphan, a widow, a self-supporting mother of three children. Traveling solo in Africa for her work, living in tents among the wildlife, taking small planes, open jeeps. No parents, no husband, the full measure of responsibility on her watch. Had she thought too much of danger as a young mother with the world imploding around her, she would have crawled under the covers in her four-poster and called 911.

Help. Three unattended children. Take them to good homes.

She followed Nicolas up the hill to the lodge.

"My idea is that you're in the lead canoe with Thomas and Oona in the center," Nicolas was saying. "I'm in the back with Venus and supplies, and Jesse is with Rosie." He grabbed her hand since the hill was slippery with mud. "And if you think Rosie can paddle a canoe, you are even more deluded than I thought."

The lights were out in Mr. Blake's office, so he must have closed up shop, it being nearly dark and a wind picking up.

"Well . . ." Georgie said drifting off, uneasy with Nicolas when he was in a mood.

He was given to short bursts of temper or biting sarcasm, even as a boy, a fatherless boy in a houseful of girls, with a mother in charge.

"Well?"

"Did I tell you that it was actually a Tuesday, June 17 in 1941, when my mother was killed at Missing Lake. And tomorrow, June 17, 2008, is also a Tuesday."

A light wind blew her hair across her face and she piled it in a clip on top of her head.

"Serendipity," she said.

"Miraculous," Nicolas replied, his irritation evident.

"I'm not suggesting it's *miraculous,* Nicolas, but it is an interesting coincidence."

Mr. Blake was standing beside Rosie, seated with the rest of the family at a round table in the lodge.

"We were just checking the river," Nicolas said.

"A little frisky tonight," Mr. Blake said. "There might be a storm."

"Let's say there's a storm," Nicolas said. "and we're in our tents at the campsite. What happens?"

"The river police patrol in their boats starting around seven in the morning when the sun is up."

"What about cell phone service?"

"Nada!" Mr. Blake said. "If you run into trouble in the night, you have to wait it out 'til morning. But there are two, sometimes three, boats patrolling the Bone every day. We haven't had a problem for four, maybe five years, but you're in the wilderness from here on out."

"No cell phone," Nicolas said shaking his

head. "Nightmare."

"What about the storm tonight?" Rosie asked.

"It's called for tomorrow — a possibility of lightning midday. If that's the case, you could stay here another night and wait for the weather to clear. Weather is usual in this part of Wisconsin."

"We can't," Georgie said quickly. "We have to be at Missing Lake on the night of the seventeenth."

"But if there's a storm, I'd advise you . . ."

"We'll wait until tomorrow morning and decide if there's a storm. But the whole trip is predicated on arriving at Missing Lake tomorrow afternoon."

Nicolas shook his head, exchanging a glance with Mr. Blake.

"We'll make it to Missing Lake," Thomas said. "No worries, Georgie."

"I have no worries," she said.

Dinner was silent and tense.

Roasted chicken family style, beer and coleslaw — six tables in the lodge, strangers, no different than Georgie's group of seven, young and older, one grandfather, elderly but fit enough. Not exactly dressed as if they were at home on rivers.

"So guys," Thomas said. "All these people are going upriver tomorrow and they look excited."

"Expert canoeists, all of them, you can tell," Venus said. "I bet they canoe four times a week."

"No one canoes four times a week," Thomas said.

"Whatever," Jesse said. "I hate canoes."

"My personal plan is to lie on my back and look at the sky rolling by," Venus said.

"You'll be paddling bow, Venus, looking straight ahead at the river and there'll be no room service," Nicolas said.

"I'm actually really scared," Rosie said. "I didn't sign up for trouble."

"Well, I did," Thomas said.

Georgie was quiet, resting her chin in her hand, looking off into the middle distance.

At the bar, a couple was kissing.

"Yuck," Jesse said.

"Don't look at them if they offend you, Jesse," Nicolas said.

"I can't help it," Jesse said. "The woman keeps staring at us."

Georgie looked over at the bar. The woman, tall, dark, curly hair, was standing on one foot, half off the stool, her hand on the man's crotch, the other around a glass of beer. The woman turned and stared at Georgie.

"She's drunk," Nicolas said. "Or crazy."

"How do you know?" Jesse asked.

"I know."

"Don't stare," Georgie said. "We'll embarrass her."

"She's not the kind of woman who embarrasses," Nicolas said.

After dinner, late, Nicolas, himself a little drunk, corralled the others to stay with him at the bar while Georgie took Oona up to a third-floor bedroom. She climbed into the double bed, still in her clothes, Oona's body pressed close, her soft curls silky on Georgie's cheek, her eyes half-closed.

Occasionally, as was happening now, Georgie would find herself staring at Oona unaware, as if to cross some mysterious boundary between them — as if there were no lines of demarcation and what Georgie saw or wished to see in Oona was herself.

Herself at four years old believing in the mercy of the world.

"Does Oona know why we are taking this trip?" Georgie asked Nicolas in the van on the way to Blake's.

"*I* don't know why we're taking this trip, Georgie."

"I wonder if she knows what murder means?" she asked. "I certainly haven't told her. Have you?"

"I haven't told her because she hasn't

59

asked. I operate on your terms."

"But certainly she's heard the word tossed around the house enough."

"Either she doesn't know or she isn't curious enough to ask. The word *fuck* is interesting to children. *Murder* not so much."

Georgie was quiet — thinking of herself, how long it was before she actually understood what had happened at Missing Lake, how long before she recognized that among her friends in Ann Arbor, her childhood had been unusual.

Georgie dimmed the light on the side table and opened the map of the Bone River charted from the canoe launch to Camp Minnie HaHa. The river curled in an S, and Missing Lake was more than halfway to the camp on the top left curve of the S, a crescent of land, not large but deep, surrounded by a pine forest noted by tiny inverted V's with a single line for the trunks.

According to the description of the murder scene in the *Chicago Tribune,* June 21, 1941, there had been four canoes pulled over the bank and out of the water. And four tents. James Willow had been in a single tent furthest from the water. Roosevelt, with his mother, had been in a tent closest to the water; the camp nurse married to the swimming counselor had been in a tent with

Georgie. Her father and mother had been in a double tent parallel to James and closest to the spot where Josephine Grove's body was discovered.

Georgie loved maps. She loved the sense they gave of permanence, as if what appeared on the map had existed through centuries of life on earth, of weather and shifts in the earth's tectonic plates, of vegetation living and dying, of animal sacrifice and human traffic. As a child, she used to play *dig your way to China, from Ann Arbor, Michigan, to Shanghai.*

As an anthropologist, she liked to believe that occurrences that had taken place on a single spot of earth remained more or less in the same topography, so the earth contained its own mysterious layered history. It was up to the present to peel away the layers into the past.

If she were present at the actual place, it was at least possible that some kind of revelation might occur in real time — memory of what had happened, as if memory, like matter, is mutable but indestructible.

"Magical thinking," Nicolas had said when Georgie explained what she hoped would happen when she arrived at the place where her mother had died.

Oona curled into her body, her arm flopped over Georgie's belly, and in the dim light from the lamp, Georgie looked at her sweet and open face, her lips turned up as if she were dreaming in smiles.

Four years old, Georgie thought, an undercurrent of emotion sweeping through her blood.

This child is four years old.

Just this last summer in Botswana, there was a problem with a monkey. The monkey, a very small monkey, had taken off against Lale's new baby boy, swaddled in cloth, next to his mother's feet. It happened every morning, and Georgie, in the next hut, heard the chattering before dawn and woke to see the monkey heckling the baby. She'd jump branch to branch on a jacaranda tree in full bloom, dropping to the ground next to the child, screaming at him in her high squabbly monkey voice, chasing back and forth, back and forth, across his line of vision. But the baby was too young to see, and the mother of the baby shouted at the monkey and threw sticks and stones, and finally Georgie took the baby into her own hut and set him high on a table.

The monkey went crazy. Charged the hut and, armed with speed and fury, flew across the entrance while Georgie stood guard. A vervet monkey with a tufted gray head, gray body and a black face, a social mammal, often used to study the behavior patterns of humans and known among scientists for her alarm calls in situations of perceived danger.

This monkey was out of control.

Georgie wondered about rabies — infrequent in Botswana except with dogs, very occasionally monkeys — but rabid is how the monkey was behaving.

She motioned to Lale, not wishing to leave her post at the entrance to the hut, and the mother looked over, her eyes blank. She made no effort to get up.

"Rabies?" Georgie asked.

The mother shook her head.

"Death," she said. "Monkey smell death."

Georgie turned away into the darkness of the hut, leaning over the baby who lay still and swaddled on the table. His tiny face was in repose, his eyes closed. Of course they would be closed — sinking is how he looked, folding into himself, no evidence of life in his face, but he was breathing. Irregular breathing? She checked. Slow breathing with barely perceptible hesitations, as if the effort to breathe was not worth the trouble.

And then he died, just stopped breathing

without a shudder as Georgie was watching him.

There and gone.

Her children had come upstairs from the bar. She heard them chatting in the corridor, doors opening and closing, Venus and Rosie in the room together, Nicolas with the boys.

Outside her bedroom door, Nicolas was on the cell phone with Olivia.

"Nothing is going to happen, Olivia," he said in a rising stage whisper. "Count on it. Two days and then we'll be home. Safe and sound."

"Hush," Venus called out loud from the room next door to Georgie's. "There are people trying to sleep."

"Oona will be fucking fine, Olivia," Nicolas was saying. "She's sleeping with Georgie. I'm here. Rosie. Venus for what that's worth. Please, Olivia. Get a grip."

Oona was on her back now, her fingers wrapped around the Hudson Bay wool blanket under her chin. She took hold of Georgie's wrist.

"Georgie?" she whispered. "What does *fucking fine* mean?"

"It means you will be fine Oona, Just fine. Nothing at all to worry about."

■ ■ ■ ■

Of course Nicolas was on edge. All of her children were, but especially Nicolas, who was always on edge, and now since he had joined the Obama press team, there were expectations unlike any he had as a lawyer at the *Washington Post.*

Tonight was the beginning of a trip her children had *not* chosen to take. They agreed to come only for Georgie, who believed in her instincts in spite of her children's reservations, in spite of her own uneasiness.

Tomorrow they would travel upriver, paddling to Missing Lake on an adventure that could change their lives.

Ever the optimist, Georgie, Nicolas had said to her.

She had almost fallen asleep — Oona breathing softly beside her — when Nicolas came up the wooden steps, walked past her room and knocked on the door to Rosie and Venus' room.

"Good news, comrades," he called. "The bartender says a storm is coming tomorrow. Hot in the morning and then all hell breaks loose."

From the Memoir of Thomas Davies

(FOR PUBLICATION)

We are a small family traveling the Bone River in northern Wisconsin on our way to a place we have never been, called Home — traveling by canoe. I am in the lead canoe paddling stern, and in the bow is Georgie who planned this trip and gave it to us with the requirement that we come. No one, not my Uncle Nicolas or my Aunt Venus — her favorite choice for a name change — or my dreamy mother or either of the cousins, wanted to come except for me, but they didn't have the heart to tell Georgie.

I wanted to come on this trip enough for all of us.

On the floor of our canoe in her little red life jacket spreading banana on my bare leg is Oona, my uncle Nicolas' daughter, and although she is only four, she is the person in the world I love completely and it worries me to think I love her enough to lose her.

If that were to happen, I would die.

I think of death (and I think about death all the time) as flat without any curves or indentations. A long perfectly straight line, which I imagine when I'm sitting in Mr. Johnson's English class and he's telling us about roses blooming in his mouth when he thinks about poetry and I hope he won't think about poetry until after the bell rings.

We are paddling in three canoes and arriving exactly now, still daylight at Missing Lake, Wisconsin, the place where we will spend the night before we reach our destination.

Now Georgie is raising her paddle in the air pointing to a cove shaped like a saucer with high pines surrounding a crescent of sandless beach. She motions for me to turn us toward shore.

Here we are!

Here is where my great-grandfather William killed his wife on the 17th of June, 1941. Or *confessed* to killing her as Georgie says. She believes that by taking this trip, *re-enacting,* she calls it, we will discover "evidence to the contrary" that her father, in spite of his confession, did not kill his wife. Georgie is an anthropologist who spends her life researching in order to discover what has been lost so that it can be found. That is how my mother describes her work.

Which is why I am keeping a journal so that thousands of years from now another anthropologist, someone like Georgie, will uncover the journal from layers and layers of earth where it has been buried. And read it and know that we, seven of us, were here on this Bone River in the town of Missing Lake on the planet earth.

Georgie likes what she calls Planned Co-incidence.

"The stars must be in alignment, but you can miss them if you don't pay attention," she says.

And taking the stars into account, she makes a plan.

"What a coincidence that Oona should be exactly the same age as I was when my mother was killed," she told us all at Christmas. "That Thomas will be thirteen, which is close to the same age as Roosevelt Mc-Crary in 1941 and so we will plan to travel on the same days that my parents were traveling sixty-seven years ago up the same Bone River to the same destination."

"And then what?" Uncle Nicolas asked at Christmas dinner.

"Then, by following these signs, these tell-

68

ing signs, we may have a chance to discover what really happened at Missing Lake, Wisconsin, on June 17, 1941."

That is how Georgie speaks. Not all the time, but occasionally with emphasis, as if she holds some kind of key to the unknown and if we stick with her, we'll discover it too.

The unknown, that is.

"Why now, Georgie?" Uncle Nicolas asked. "You've had more than sixty years since your father died to find out what happened."

"Because, *now* is when I want to know."

In the second canoe, my mother Rosie is paddling stern in that sleepy way she has of doing everything. So the canoe keeps heading for the bank on the opposite side of the river because she lets the paddle laze in one direction.

I can hear my cousin Jesse over the whistle of wind. "Rosie," he shouts. "Pay fucking attention."

Jesse is too old to say *fuck* in every sentence, but that is what he does. And I want to kill him when he yells at her.

Our whole family is on this trip except the cats and our dog, Kubla, a retriever, who was given to me last Christmas as a substitute for my father, who died two years ago in August. Kubla Khan. Uncle Nicolas' choice of a name.

When we got Kubla, I begged my mother to name him for my father and I wish she had been willing. My father loved dogs, and if a dog had his name, which was Richard Davies, he would still be alive.

"Richard," I would call going to the back door. "Come here, Richard Davies. Dinner is ready."

And he would come wagging his tail, and I would give him dinner and sit down on the floor of the kitchen with him while he ate.

Richard Davies captured in the brave heart of our dog.

But my mother said *No,* under no circumstances. It's disrespectful, Thomas, and nothing, not even your father's name shouted from the mountaintops, can make a difference now. And certainly not his name on a dog.

I love my mother very much, but it is difficult to get her attention — as if when she looks at me, she sees not me — *and I know she loves me* — but a painting she is imagining on the inside of her eyelids. For that is what she does. Paint, and she is known for it and her work is in museums even though she's only forty-three. And pretty. She is very pretty and kind of fairylike, floating through a room.

But there are *no* people in her art work, only rooms, bedrooms with the sheets tossed half off the bed as if someone has just left and is brushing his teeth in a bathroom next door, a dining room, food on the table, a wineglass turned over, chairs pulled back, napkins on the floor, a living room with a book facedown on the couch, a chair leaning against the wall, a painting crooked, something disturbing as if a fight happened in that room and the people who had been fighting left.

Uncle Nicolas is in the last canoe and paddling alone since Aunt Venus is sleeping in the bottom of the canoe because that is what she does on family trips. Sleep.

We'll only be gone two days because Nicolas is on the traveling press corps for Barack Obama's campaign to be president of the United States and has to work 24/7 as he says. We are all very excited about Barack Obama and what his election will mean and what he believes in and what he will do for the country. And I am also excited but mainly to be invited to the White House to have dinner with Sasha and Malia and Michelle and even the president if he gets to be president.

"I'm sure we can arrange something, Thomas," Uncle Nicolas says.

So having dinner with Barack Obama is a little like this trip. Maybe I will find out that Georgie's father did murder her mother. Or maybe that he didn't. Either way, I will have a story to tell when I go back to school in the fall.

My father told me not long before he died that I should take care of my eyes. He was sitting in a chair in the hospital in Chicago next to a window overlooking the beautiful city, and by then he was a little fuzzy, his words spoken as if through the thickness of vanilla pudding, but "Thomas," he said. "Take care of your eyes because *you* can see things that other people don't. Most people are very poor at looking. Your mother, for example, is a painter, but what she sees is in her imagination. What Georgie sees is in her past. And what you see is here."

What I have discovered already by looking at people is that nothing is normal. Most people are stranger than they seem to be and you never know what to expect of them, even of yourself.

I should let you know, although you probably can already tell, that I'm not a regular thirteen-year-old kid absorbed like water into the center of the group. For starters — ever since my father died, I have had a speech problem that Georgie says is *nerves* and the doctor says is a speech problem. I begin a perfectly normal sentence and five words out, maybe six or seven, I can't speak. I see the sentence on the screen of my brain rolling out word after word just as I planned it, but nothing. Silence.

So now I'm in acting classes playing Malvolio in *Twelfth Night* in the summer children's theater when I get back home.

"If you memorize someone else's words instead of making up your own, maybe you'll be able to speak sentence to sentence ..."

At least that was my mother's idea in sending me to acting classes.

Which I love. Which are the best part of my life. Nothing could be better than being someone who I am not.

When I was little, maybe three or four, I fell in love with dinosaurs. I could spend day after day lying on my stomach in the living room of our apartment in Chicago reading dinosaur books or playing with the dino-

73

saurs my father had bought me at the Natural History Museum. Or dreaming about them.

Until I understood extinction. And then for weeks and months I would lie in my bed, the covers drawn up to my eyes, alert to changes in the atmosphere around us which might announce the arrival of extinction.

I was heartbroken for the dinosaurs, apologizing to each one — the diplodocus, the triceratops, the stegosaurus — as if I were in some way responsible. But that gave way to a terrifying fear for my family and me.

If those huge and powerful beasts roaming the same earth on which we live could disappear, what did that mean for me and my mother and my father and the rest of us, and I told my parents one night at bedtime that I thought it a good idea not to have any more children.

"If you never become alive," I explained to them, "there is nothing of you to disappear."

I was ten when my father died of brain cancer on the morning of August 20, 2006, just before school started. I *knew* he was going to die. Everyone had told me — my mother and Uncle Nicolas and Venus and even Georgie, who does not believe that children should be left without hope. Georgie explained that they told me the truth about my father so I would be prepared for his death when it happened.

But I was not.

■ ■ ■ ■

MISSING LAKE

■ ■ ■ ■

June 17, 2008

GEORGIANNA

In the bow, paddling lead of the three canoes, Georgie is losing the rhythm — *dip swing, dip swing, dip swing* — she reminds herself, her mind caught up in what is to come.

"Georgie!" Thomas shouts from the stern. "Paddle. You keep forgetting."

"Got it," she calls back, lifting her thumb in the air.

Ahead, the river is black and calm, the sun above the tree line but falling in the West — no longer hot as it has been all day. High clouds roll across the northern horizon, but there is no rumble of weather in the air, no atmospheric change announcing trouble. They are close to Missing Lake, where they will spend the night, and the storm has not arrived.

Will not arrive, Georgie is thinking,

Ahead there's a bend in the river, the bank curving into the S shape of a cove, and she sees the crescent of Missing Lake as they paddle around the circle of land, a large sign in the distance although she cannot read the letters.

"Here we are!" she calls out to Thomas, lifting her paddle, pointing in the direction of land.

In shallow water, muddy under foot, Georgie throws her leg over the side of the canoe and climbs out, both hands on the gunnel to steady herself, conscious that her family is watching for any sign that she will — as Rosie had put it just that morning — *fall apart.*

She is small, with long brown hair — a dusting of white — piled loosely on her head and secured with combs that will regularly fall out to make a comb path to the water by the time they leave Missing Lake.

"Don't scatter, Georgie," Rosie said earlier as they put in their canoes from the outfitters' launch. "You know, don't fall apart."

Scattering is what happens when she takes on more than she can do — her wallet lost, her keys tossed accidentally in the trash, her sweater on inside out, a marked-up student dissertation left at the coffee shop. Not often but lately.

"Of course I won't fall apart, babes," she

said, surprised that Rosie of all her pre-occupied children, trapped in their own emotional worlds of profit and loss, would notice her mother's distraction.

At seventy — seventy! It is difficult to believe. She wants to be seen by her children as the small, agile, resilient mother she has always been. Which is why she grabs the gunnel so she won't fall — not apart but down, and falling down would be, for them, another kind of loss.

Or maybe not. *Not* has occurred to her. It is altogether possible that they are ready for her to actually die. Ready — just that — not hoping or even thinking it is time or that enough is enough. But practically speaking — and Georgie is a surprisingly practical woman in spite of herself — her death might be for them a kind of freedom.

Out of the back pocket of her hiking shorts she pulls the topographical map she picked up from the outfitters in Riverton.

Her grandfather had hung maps of Michigan in the main entrance to their home in Ann Arbor, seven of them from the first recorded map of Michigan before it became a state — *very valuable,* he'd told her.

She had asked him if he could draw from memory a map of Camp Minnie HaHa.

My home, she'd said.

Ann Arbor is your home, Georgianna, he replied.

But he was mistaken.

The night before at the lodge, unable to sleep, Oona beside her, Georgie had filled in the crescent at Missing Lake as she remembered it from the newspaper stories describing the discovery of her mother's body — a stand of pines where her mother had been found, lowland craggy brush with exposed roots between the river and the pine forest where the tents were pitched. A jagged shoreline. It gave her a sense of order to draw the tents, each with a different-colored pencil — she wrote the names of the occupants in red ballpoint on the side of the map as the *Chicago Tribune* had listed them.

"Pull the canoe up onto the bank and follow me," Georgie calls out to Thomas.

"Bring Oona."

She stands with her back to the river, rough this early evening splashing against the muddy shoreline.

Perhaps a storm is coming, a drop in temperature, an odd calm promising change.

In Washington, calm announced a storm but the temperature would be hotter, the air heavy. Georgie knew to be close to cover. Storms could be treacherous and quick. Especially the tree-lined streets of Washington, a shallow root system, the wide limbs, weighted with leaves, branches growing around the electrical wires.

But she doesn't know the weather in northern Wisconsin.

River weather.

She puts her hand in the pocket of her shorts and pops a caramel in her mouth.

Too late to worry about what she has not planned. Which is nothing, simply nothing, so fixed has she been on her destination.

The sign for Missing Lake is wooden, the letters burned intaglio and painted black, freshly painted. It could not have been the same sign that had been there in 1941, but was it in the same place, she wonders, looking to the left at the bank rising to a stand of pine trees, a small clearing, a red wheelbarrow.

A wheelbarrow for what?

Nine people were present at the catastrophe (she prefers the word *catastrophe,* which seems more accidental than *crime,* although *crime* was the word used in the newspaper reports and by her grandparents). She had read the *Chicago Tribune* story of June 21,

1941, where the nine were listed by name and age:

William Grove, age 37
Josephine Grove, age 33
Girl Child Grove, age 4
James Willow, age 21
Adelaide Merry, age 32
Roderick Brown, age 30
Alicia Brown, age 29
Clementine McCrary, age 33
Boy Child McCrary, age 11

In the article, the McCrarys were identified as Negroes.
There were two Negroes, mother and son.
"I wonder why they called them Negroes?" Georgie had asked her grandmother at the time.

"Because they *were* Negroes — that is a classification of race and we are Caucasian, which means white people," her grandmother had said. "It was unusual for Negroes to be going to a camp in northern Wisconsin where there were Indians but not black-skinned people."

"Is that bad?"

"Not good or bad," her grandmother said. "Just a fact."

"And did you know those Negroes?"

"I saw them when I came to pick you up at Missing Lake after the crime. But I didn't *know* them or anything about them."

Georgie walks up the steep hill to a circle of high pine trees just above the sign for Missing Lake. In the distance, Rosie's canoe appears to be trapped among tree roots extending from the far shore line across the river

Nicolas calls out instructions: "For chrissake, Rosie, get out of the canoe so you can help Jesse free it up," he shouts.

Georgie wishes Nicolas were not so short-tempered and critical, as if growing up in a family of women had entitled him to take charge.

"It's too rough," Rosie calls.

"You'll be fine," Nicolas says. "Just *do* it."

"I *can't!*"

The canoe tips perilously close to capsizing as Rosie slips over the side and sinks into the water, her hands gripping the top of the boat. With Jesse on the other side, she swims the rocking boat away from the bank and into current that has picked up speed.

"Kick!" Nicolas shouts and, shaking his fist at his mother, calls at the top of his voice,

"God, Georgie, what a crazy idea this trip is."

Thomas is standing by the water, holding the rope attached to the bow of his canoe, his eyes fixed on the top of his mother's bobbing head.

"Are you guys okay?" Nicolas calls.

"They can't hear you," Thomas says, watching his mother, her face in the water. Underwater and up and then it seems as if they are swimming out of the current — her hand in the air, her thumb up.

"Jesus, Rosie!" Nicolas says as she climbs out of the canoe. "You are impossibly stubborn."

Georgie is walking toward the spot she has marked on her map, careful not to trip, rocky on the shoreline, a rise from the river, the land flat for a short distance, a pine needle bed, the soil sandy — and then an incline, heavy with tree roots and the sign MISSING LAKE.

If her mother had been discovered just to the left of the sign — as indicated in the newspaper reports — lying in the root bed of pine trees at the high level of the hill, then Georgie is very close to where it happened.

She's athletic, walking every day or at the

gym, swing dancing at Glen Echo Park on Saturday nights. Young for seventy — everyone says so. Not that her face is unwrinkled, because it is wrinkled. But because of her body, which is slender and quick. She never stops moving.

"She doesn't take pills," Venus has said with admiration since Venus would happily take any pills offered, never mind the number, so she notices that kind of thing.

Thomas pulls the canoe out of the water and picks Oona up in his arms, her legs wrapped tight around his waist. Ahead, Georgie has stopped, her hands in her pockets, her head down as if something on the ground has captured her attention.

"What's Georgie doing?" Oona asks.

"Maybe she is praying."

"Praying?"

"Praying for all of us to be fine and have fun and good times.

"Is something bad going to happen now?"

"It's dinnertime," Thomas says. "We'll eat dinner."

"What will we eat?"

"Hamburgers and beans."

"But I don't like hamburgers and beans."

"Of course you don't."

"Mama is a vegetarian."

"But she isn't here, so you can eat hamburgers and beans."

"Are we going to sleep in the canoe?"

"We're going to sleep in a tent in sleeping bags, and we'll build a fire to cook the hamburgers and beans and to keep us warm."

"Good," Oona says. "I'll sleep in the sleeping bag with you."

Georgie hasn't moved.

It occurs to Thomas that she might be crying, because she *should* be crying. They have come to the place where her mother was strangled and he is holding Oona who is four, so Georgie must feel she is still four, as if no time at all has passed since her mother died and four is as old as she will ever get to be.

At least, Thomas thinks, that is how he would feel if he were Georgie.

"Do you think we're here?" Thomas asks, aching to pee.

"I do," Georgie replies.

"Then where are we?" Thomas asks.

"Exactly here," Georgie says, halfway up the incline, leaning forward not to fall.

She would like to believe that she is at the precise place, the small circle of earth where her mother had been sitting when the killer walked up the incline. Maybe it was early morning, not yet light — maybe the middle of the night and her mother had come here away from the tents not to wake anyone, unable to sleep. The night had a full moon, so it may as well have been day — and the killer came, not from nowhere, not some stranger out of the forest, but *one* among the nine.

Likely her mother was expecting nothing from the killer — a conversation, even a gesture of affection. Nothing that would have concerned her or caused her to call out.

And then quickly, in a flash of movement, maybe with a struggle, maybe not — her mother had been fragile, unwell since a stillborn boy the year after Georgie was born. Not emotionally well either for reasons Georgie had never been able to piece together.

There was a rope and the *someone* wound it quickly around her mother's neck and tightened it and held it at that tension until she could no longer breathe.

Georgie had read the article about her father's confession from the front page of the *Chicago Tribune,* June 21, 1941. Her grandmother gave it to her four years after her father's death in prison from pneumonia.

"Overcome by an uncontrollable rage," he was reported as saying.

"At your wife?" he was asked.

"At myself," he said.

"And why was that?" he was asked.

But he had nothing to add to his testimony except his deep and agonizing sorrow.

"Do you believe this is true?" Georgie had asked her grandmother.

"What part?"

"That he killed her? Is that part true."

"I don't know," her grandmother replied, stroking the back haunches of the tabby cat sitting in her lap.

"What else did my father say?"

"That's all he ever said. Nothing more to the lawyers or to the police. He confessed and they accepted his confession."

"I don't believe he killed her," Georgie had said.

"That is your choice, my lamb," her grandmother said. "The only necessary belief you must hold in your heart is a belief in God."

"I do," Georgie said, although she didn't know what she believed except to wonder *why* if God had been taking care of His children, had He not taken better care of Georgianna Grove.

"I wanted you to read the newspaper

article for yourself," her grandmother said. "And now you have."

"Front page of the *Chicago Tribune* because the camp was well known in Chicago," her grandfather said, a measured man not much given to conversation. "Boys went there from Chicago . . ." He paused. "What happened didn't do the reputation of the camp much good."

Right before Roosevelt's letter arrived at the Home for the Incurables but before the end of the first semester of classes, a kind of strangeness overtook Georgie's mind. Not all the time but occasionally like a wave of nausea. The first time it happened she was on her way to the university, thinking about the lecture she was giving that afternoon when turbulence erupted — that's how it felt — an eruption — moments out of her life swimming through her brain. A friend from grammar school with ringlets, a small scene at a dress store with her grandmother, who insisted Georgie must wear plaid to church, a green velvet chair from her bedroom in Ann Arbor, her grandmother in an open casket at the Walker Funeral Home, turned not faceup but on her stomach and covered with a quilt.

At 21st and G, she pulled the car over to

the side of the road and got out, leaving the engine running, and walked up and down the sidewalk until the movie reel ceased its hysteria through her brain and disappeared.

And then on the night of her seventieth birthday, after she had announced to her family's unhappiness the gift of a canoe trip up the Bone River to meet Roosevelt Mc-Crary, it happened again.

She was in bed in the large four-poster that had belonged to her parents — *she never should have kept it* — lying on her back, warm with desire, as often happened to her, at ease with a sense of well-being, falling into a soft sleep, and Charley — she had called him Charles then — was standing in the hall of her grandparents' house in Ann Arbor, his head against the green grapevine wallpaper, reaching his hands down the back of her skirt, pulling her into his body, his tongue hot and silky in her mouth.

Then he was gone. Gone and she couldn't catch hold of the memory of him, only the sadness of unfulfilled desire.

All of the men in her life had left it.

She got out of bed, turned on the side light, opened the door to her bedroom and started down the stairs when Rosie stepped out of the bathroom.

"Georgie. It's after midnight," Rosie had said. "Are you okay?"

"Of course I'm okay," she said, always fine for her children. "I'm just going downstairs to make a cup of tea."

"But Mama —" Rosie said with genuine concern. "What happened to your nightgown?"

Georgie stood at the top of the stairs and looked down. She must have been in a light sleep instead of a waking erotic dream and taken off her nightgown.

She smiled at Rosie. "It's after one, darling," she said to her daughter. "You should go to bed." She took hold of the bannister. "Goodnight, my sweet."

And she continued down the stairs to the kitchen as if it had been her plan all along to walk naked through the house to get a cup of tea.

Georgie had never seen a therapist when she was a child. Therapy would not have occurred to her midwestern grandparents, hardworking Protestants who were clear about mental health. There was no such thing as "mental illness." A person was crazy or not. Nothing ambiguous about the mind.

Stiff upper lip, her grandfather would say.

Pull yourself up by your bootstraps. Look on the bright side.

"You're a lucky girl to have the temperament you have," her grandmother had told her. "A sunny disposition just like me."

Sometimes Georgie would lie in her small single bed under the eaves on the third floor, close to the stars, covered with the quilt her grandmother had made from her mother's old dresses thinking how amazing it was that even though her mother was murdered and her father had maybe killed her (but probably not) and was in any case dead — here was Georgie — eleven, twelve, thirteen . . . a perfectly ordinary girl and even popular and well liked and quite pretty. All the things regarded as necessary for happiness.

And was she happy?

Of course she was.

The story she told herself about her mother's death was the story her grandparents had suggested she tell. It was the story they told to their friends and neighbors, as if Georgie's father's confession were unknown to the people in Ann Arbor.

Her mother was murdered on a canoe trip where the family was headed to open the boy's camp and her father had died of pneumonia.

"You have to have a better story," Charley told her after he knew what had happened. "Or else tell the truth."

"I don't know the truth."

"You can say that. You can tell people you don't know the truth."

Nicolas and Jesse are building a fire, close to the water, the only land flat enough for safety although Rosie suggests the hill where there is softer seating.

"You should've been a girl scout, Rosie," Nicolas says. "You'd have been terrific."

Rosie has changed clothes from her swim and sits near the fire wrapped in a towel, another towel around her wet hair. She is small like her mother, with delicate hands and feet, small-featured too, a childlike way about her; although since Richard's death, she has aged, her eyes have a kind of film over the pupils, the brightness of blue gone, the rose color of her skin for which she was named, faded. Her family notices these things, but she does not seem to. She doesn't talk about the loss of Richard, doesn't mention sadness. She has always been distracted by nature, off in another place, and so she is distracted now.

They pitch the tents on higher land away from the water but too close to the trees to build a fire there. Three tents, one large, sleeping bags.

Thomas with Oona. The women together in the large tent. Jesse with Nicolas.

"You and me, Oona," Thomas says. "Bliss."

"What is bliss?" Oona asks.

"It's happiness and that's what we're going to have on this trip."

"Then why is Jesse so bad tempered?"

"Not his kind of trip," Thomas says. "Jesse likes life as usual."

They are sitting on the hill watching the hamburgers over the fire, Nicolas cooking, Venus laying out the plastic forks and paper plates and napkins, baked beans and fruit, lemonade and cookies. She opens a bottle of wine, pours lemonade for herself and the children.

Through the trees they watch the sun sinking in the west — rolling patterns of leaves in shadows tumble across the bank, dim patches of light on the river, the waves breaking in crescents across the surface.

Downstream, the wind sounds a low roar.

"Do you think we're going to have a storm?" Georgie asks Nicolas.

"A storm is predicted," he says "I told you that. Hot during the day and then all hell breaks loose."

"What does that mean?" Venus asks.

"A bad storm," Georgie says. "Are you sure?"

"Who knows what a bad storm is here. Some kind of storm," Nicolas says. "I for one don't like Wisconsin, so I'd rather not end my life here."

"We should secure the tents," Venus says, her legs apart, her hands on her hips, the tone of her voice thoughtful. "Move them closer to the trees in a sheltered spot?"

Nicolas looks over at the high pines whining in the wind, their trunks supple. Hard to guess if a strong wind could take them down. He is anxious and lights a cigarette.

"I'd bet on a clearing," he says. "That one over there, without such high trees."

He reaches into the pocket of his shorts and takes out his vibrating cell.

"You know this trip is crazy, Georgie, traveling up the river like we know what we're doing."

He steps away from the fire and checks the phone.

"I've got a call," he calls out.

"Yes? Are you there?" he says. "Can you hear me?"

"Shit!" He hits at the air with his fist. "No go! I thought fucking Verizon worked everywhere. You told me I'd have reception with Verizon here."

"I said I thought you would."

"And that Mr. Blake guy told you there would be *no* reception," Venus says.

"There's probably an emergency at the Obama headquarters, and how will I know what's going on for the next twenty-four hours." He flips the hamburgers. "I assume there's a land line at the camp so if there's a disaster, I can find out when we get there."

"There are a trillion other people on Obama's campaign besides you, Nicolas," Venus says. "How could there be a disaster?"

"Anything's possible. Iraq, something racial — we worry about that stuff. The Republicans are back on the 'Is Obama an American?' story."

He picks up a cup of wine and drinks it down.

"Dad," Jesse says. "Cool it. We're in the wilderness. There's nothing we can do."

"You'll be whistling another tune, Jesse, if the emergency happens to be here at the glorious campsite of Missing Lake."

They gather around the fire, wrapping blankets around their shoulders, over their heads. Their faces peer out at the darkness like turtles. Oona falls asleep on Georgie's knees and Thomas on his stomach on a blanket, his feet resting in Rosie's lap, his chin in his fists.

"Should we sing?" Venus asks.

"God no, please Venus. No singing," Nicolas says.

"But here we are at the place where Georgie's mother was murdered," Thomas is saying. "This is a big deal so we need to talk."

"In the big deal category, this registers about a two," Jesse says.

"It's a big deal for Georgie," Thomas says. "If someone you love dies, he dies again and again for the rest of your life. That is what I think."

The wind picks up in gusty intervals — the sky seems less ominous, the fire bright enough for them to see each other as shapes in the darkness. A comfortable silence falls over the night.

"What do you really want to discover on this trip, Georgie?" Nicolas asks.

"More than I know now," Georgie says. "I grew up as if my parents had never been. No one I have met seems to remember them as anything more than crime fiction."

"But Roosevelt?" Nicolas asked. "I mean this guy is almost eighty, maybe even with a little dementia."

"She wants to find out whether her father killed her mother," Thomas says. "Pretty simple."

"You're excited to find that out too, Thomas," Nicolas says.

"I am."

"After all this time, Georgie, what difference will it really make?" Nicolas asks.

"It makes a difference to me," Thomas says.

Venus wraps her sleeping bag around her shoulders.

"Georgie's looking for the originals," she says.

"I thought *we* were the originals," Nicolas replies, crouching next to the fire.

"Home is what she calls Camp Minnie HaHa," Venus says. "Always since we were young, she has told us that."

"Is that true, Georgie?" Rosie loops her arm over Thomas' shoulders. "You were only four years old."

"It's where she went the first year she was born," Thomas says.

"December 17, 1937. Scorpio, rising Taurus, etcetera, etcetera."

"Please, Venus!" Nicolas says. "Spare the stars."

He gets up, opens a can of beer and checks his cell phone.

"News from the front line?" Venus asks.

"What is the front line?" Thomas asks.

"We are," Venus says.

Nicolas slips into the circle next to his mother, the fire warm on their cheeks.

"Georgie." His voice drops assuming a quiet detachment. "Since we're all here and soon we'll be there at the camp and it's not likely we're going to turn back at this point, I want to ask you . . ."

"We want to know about Roosevelt," Rosie says quickly

"What about Roosevelt?" Georgie can hear the rising tension in her own voice.

"We think you are falling in love with him."

"With someone I don't remember and haven't seen? Who has written me once and talked to me twice since we made the decision to visit him."

She sits on her haunches, her hands in her lap.

"Since *I* made the decision," she corrects herself. "And all of you agreed to come."

"We know you, Georgie," Venus says. "We're all grown-ups now and we can see what is happening to you."

"Already you're imagining a life with Roosevelt," Rosie says.

"Not at all," Georgie says, getting up to head down the hill to her tent, but Nicolas stops her, his hand gentle on her shoulder.

Nights since Roosevelt's letter arrived, she

has put herself to sleep with scenes of him rushing across her mind — in Washington, in her large kitchen seated at the table, his feet crossed at the ankles on a chair, following her upstairs to her bedroom — in Wisconsin, in a canoe on the Bone River — playing frame to frame across her half-sleep.

What her children don't know, what she will not tell them — are the postcards Roosevelt has written to her, weekly postcards slipped into a square brown envelope, no return address. Twenty-five of them in a pocket of her backpack, concealed in a black mesh zipper bag filed by date beginning the day after Christmas 2007. Every week, usually on Thursdays, a day she does not teach, a postcard has arrived, written in his sprawling hand with a photograph on the front of Camp Minnie HaHa. Always the same photograph, taken at night from the water, probably in the fall, the lights in the lodge illuminating the trees.

"There were nine people on the first trip, right?" Nicolas speaks quietly.

Georgie nods.

"And it's very unlikely that anyone — a killer type, even now, would be camped out in the woods of Missing Lake, Wisconsin, waiting to kill strangers."

"What about the red wheelbarrow?" Thomas asks.

"What about the wheelbarrow?" Nicolas replies.

"Well somebody who has left this wheelbarrow could be around lurking in the woods."

"That wheelbarrow was probably left to decorate the campsite a month ago," Venus says.

"Decorate?" Thomas asks.

"To make the place feel homey, you know — for the likes of us arriving in our canoes to spend the night."

Venus lights a match, holds it between her fingers watching it burn down to her skin and blows it out.

"Nothing like a red wheelbarrow to create a feeling of home."

"Go on, Nicolas," Rosie says. "What were you going to say?"

Nicolas moves closer to Georgie, leans against her shoulder.

"Let's be sensible," he begins. "Why have you always refused to believe that it *was* your father in spite of the fact that he confessed?"

"Because . . . and I *have* explained this to you." Georgie rearranges her legs, her back against a slender tree trunk. She should *not* feel the need to have these discussions with her children. Her grown children. But she does. She always has.

"Because all the questions that could have been asked, the ones that might have revealed what had really gone on at Missing Lake, were not asked. My father preempted the questions."

"We know that," Rosie said.

"I have a letter he wrote to me just before he died in which he takes exception to his confession."

"Which letter?" Nicolas asks. "I only know about one letter that he wrote from prison."

"That's the only one I have," Georgie says. "*There will be more news tomorrow* is what he says."

"He was very ill when he wrote that letter," Nicolas says. "Likely delirious from fever."

"Those were his words. It was as if he were telling me he had *not* killed her and someday I would discover the person who had," Georgie says. "I believe what I believe."

"But the question is *why* if he didn't do it did he say he did?" Nicolas asks. "Unless he was protecting the person who did kill her, right?"

Georgie shrugs.

"We'll find that out when we meet Roosevelt," she says.

"So let's assume it wasn't your father," Nicolas says. "Have you wondered at all why Roosevelt wrote to you now? Out of the blue when he's never seen or contacted you before?"

"It was my birthday. He's old. I'm getting old. Lots of reasons."

"What about your sixtieth birthday?"

"Nicolas!"

"I think we have to be prepared, Georgie. I think we have to consider that Roosevelt might have been the one to kill your mother or that he knows who killed her or even knows it *was* after all your father. And he wants you to know that now. Or maybe he wants to tell you something else. But surely he wants to say something to you."

"Like what?" Georgie asks, tense now, her chin resting uneasily on her bent knees.

"I think we should be alert, that's all," Nicolas says. "You have to admit this is a very strange trip."

"I would like to understand who my father was, and Roosevelt is the only opportunity I've ever had to do that."

Later, just inside her tent, Georgie sits on top of her sleeping bag and opens her backpack in which she has hidden Roosevelt's postcards. Most nights she reads them before she goes to sleep as she has done, over and over, the same postcards, since December.

December 23, 2007
Dear G: Full moon tonight and the skunks are out meandering across the porch of the lodge doing their skunky thing. Sincerely, R

January 1, 2008
Dear G — Heading to the town of Missing Lake if I can get the truck through last night's snow. Sincerely. Happy New Year, R

January 10, 2008
Dear G, I figure if I write you every week like this, you'll get to know me better. Then we won't be strangers when we meet. Sincerely, R

By the end of March, there was a change of tone — the postcards stained with the dirty thumb print on the edges as if he read them over and over before they were mailed.
It pleased Georgie to imagine him consid-

ering and reconsidering what he has written to her.

March 29, 2008 (three postcards in one day, clipped together)

Dear Georgianna, When we returned to Washington after your mother had been killed and your father taken away, my mother got me a puppy — although she did not like dogs, Not the smell of them nor their unpredictable habits, but she got one for me, a pound dog named Mercy so I would forget about what happened at Missing Lake, Especially watching your father go off to jail. Ever since then I've had a dog who sleeps with me at the bottom of the bed, goes where I go, eats what I eat. Now Mercy. Age 14. Love, R.

Love. Georgie read that postcard again and again: *Love, R.*

April 18, 2008

Dear Georgianna, Change in the sky tonight, young spring sky coming on the horizon — and I'm lying in the cold on my back in a hammock watching the map of the heavens and thinking of you under the same sky but a southern one,

a different horizon — and not in a hammock. Love, R

She replaces them, closes her backpack
and waits.

For what is she waiting? she asks herself.
For *something* to happen? Something seems
possible, or is that sense of anticipation just
her own uneasiness?

Should she stay up all night waiting for
sunrise?

Beside her, Rosie is sound asleep. Amazing that Rosie can sleep with such abandon
on the hard ground in this unfamiliar
landscape as if the accumulation of sorrows
in her life has its own drawer which she
keeps closed.

Peering out of the open flap of the tent
into the darkness, Georgie listens to the
whistle of wind, gathering force as it moves
across the water, a strong gust through the
tent. And then in the distance, thunder.
Thunder?

Or something else.

The long, low growl of a large animal in
the forest nearby.

"Bears?" she wonders. "Would bears be
foraging at night in Missing Lake?"

■ ■ ■ ■

THE BONE RIVER

■ ■ ■ ■

June 17, 1941

WILLIAM

The weather had been stormy ever since they launched on the Bone River. Heavy rains pelting the canoes like so many stones, William soaked to the bone even with a slicker. Things were going poorly. Likely they couldn't have a fire that night when they camped at Missing Lake. Too much wetness on the ground, the twigs and branches soaked with the weight of water. Beans out of a can for dinner. Spam. *A glass of whiskey would be good,* he thought.

William was paddling stern in the lead canoe. He always paddled stern, but luckily Roosevelt was in the bow with his powerful arms. Even at eleven and a city boy. A workhorse, Roosevelt, and he was the heft in the boat making William's job of keeping them on course a lot easier than it would have been without him.

In the middle, Josephine was sitting with Georgianna between her legs — only Georgianna got to go between his wife's legs any longer.

She had gotten fat since the lost baby.

When William first saw Josie on the steps of the library at the University of Michigan, where they met, he was in his last year of coursework for a Ph.D. in physics — physics because he was good at it and new to the United States from a village in Lithuania and didn't need perfect English for physics, although he never made use of that degree.

There on the steps of the library was Josephine Hennings, slender, with almost perfect features — straight nose, wide-set eyes, full lips, high color in her cheek and red hair the color of autumn, spread like a cape over her shoulders. She had small hands like the hands of a child.

Lately he held Georgianna's hand lightly in his own just to remember what it had felt like with Josephine at the beginning.

The high cheekbones had gone to flesh, and her eyes, which were hazel, sunk to golden marbles growing smaller and smaller, only seeds for sight.

Unwell in body and soul. Depressed.

He didn't talk about depression with her family. As far as the Hennings were concerned, depression was a matter of choice.

Josephine stopped sleeping with William when Georgianna had a high fever and Josie moved into her room and stayed for weeks sleeping on a couch.

Something happened then.

In time William gathered the nerve to ask her why she didn't want to make love any longer — gently, he asked her. She was delicate and refined. Sex was likely new to her when they met — and faithful to her request, they didn't sleep together until they married — he could imagine with a girl like Josephine that sex was maybe a little dirty or messy, too many fluids coming from god knows where.

But she accustomed herself to him, not exactly willing, but available.

This last winter he had finally asked, did her distance from him have to do with something he could change, because that he would gladly do.

"Distance?" she asked.

And then he said the first thing that came to mind.

"Is it because I'm Jewish?"

William did not like Dr. and Mrs. Hennings, not from the first night he had dinner at their house. A formal dinner with a long white table cloth and silver cutlery and gold-rimmed china and bad food. It had struck him as a contradiction to go to all the trouble to dress up a table and then serve bad food. Lamb cooked to death, shards of black meat like charcoal, and vegetables boiled in water until there must have been more vegetable in the water than squished on the plate.

"So," Dr. Hennings said, "you're getting your Ph.D. in physics at our great university, I understand. You must be planning to teach at university."

"Actually not," William said. "I'm planning to run a boys' camp in Wisconsin."

When William first came to the United States, it was to live with his uncle Irving who was an American-educated physician and lived in Washington, D.C. It had been his uncle's suggestion that he apply to be the director at Camp Minnie HaHa when the notice of a search for a new director went out. A camp Irving knew well since he was one of three investors in Minnie HaHa with his two close friends in medical school at the University of Michigan, the camp where his sons had gone, where he vacationed with his family after camp closed in August.

It was Irving's thought that directing a

boys' camp would provide William with a *foothold* in America.

Given the troubles, William would not be going back to Lithuania in the near future.

Or maybe ever, Irving suggested, as tensions in Germany escalated.

"You'll be stuck here just as I've been," his uncle said. "It's not home but certainly not a bad place to live a life."

William wasn't going to be a physicist either, and if he taught at all, it would be younger boys who had not made up their minds. His job as he imagined it would be to teach them to think. To *question* was the better word.

So that's what he did. High school world history in Chicago in the winter and Camp Minnie HaHa in the summer.

When William first arrived with his uncle at the camp — the beginning of March — the long dirt road was muddy, deep potholes, streams of water pouring down the hill. At the entrance to the camp where the road opened to a wide expanse of land circled by cabins shadowed with high pines, there was a large, handmade sign painted white with black letters:

WELCOME TO CAMP MINNIE HAHA, the sign read. NO DOGS. NO JEWS.

"Something new," his uncle said. "That

115

sign wasn't here last summer when I picked up the boys. So it must be the winter folks getting a whiff of what's going on in Germany."

"I don't think I should come here to work," William said.

"Oh no, William," Irving replied. "You *should* come and make no mention of the fact that you are Jewish. Simply take down the sign."

He looped his arm through William's.

"But I wonder, don't you," his uncle said in his wry understated way, "how ever are they able to keep the dogs out, since there's no barbed-wire fence."

William had not looked forward to the conversation at the Hennings dinner table and when dinner was served, any pleasure he might have had in the evening was gone — except there was a brief exchange initiated by Mrs. Hennings that figured in his present life and had started that evening.

"So," she had asked. "You came to this country when?"

"Nineteen thirty," William replied, which was true, though much of what he told them later was not.

"From Lithuania," he added. "I came to Washington, D.C., with the intention of getting an American education to live with my uncle who came to America before the War and stayed. But my plan was always to return to Lithuania."

"Ahhhh." Dr. Hennings rested his long chin in his fist.

William realized too late — he ought to have known from Dr. Hennings' "Ahhhh" that the conversation was likely to go downhill.

"So it would be difficult for you to go back home now, I presume," Dr. Hennings said.

"We're Presbyterians," Mrs. Hennings said as if that were the conversation in play. "Do you have a religious practice?"

A religious practice, William thought. Did he have a religion?

"I don't," he said.

The *don't* was emphatic but nothing was going to stop Mrs. Hennings from executing her plan for the evening.

"Then," Mrs. Hennings said, so pleasantly William found himself wondering how the wet vegetables would look on her lavender summer frock should he choose to spill them. "You must be a cultural Jew."

"Actually," he said, weighing his love for their daughter against his hatred for them. "I am not a Jew at all. I'm a lapsed Catholic."

And that was that. He couldn't be a Protestant in Lithuania, but he could be a Catholic.

They married the following summer, June 1936, in Ann Arbor at the First Presbyterian Church and went on a honeymoon on the Bone River to spend the summer with seventy-five young boys between the ages of eight and seventeen.

Behind his canoe, William could hear Clementine's low bluesy voice, and it sounded as if she were arguing with James. All he could hear from James — the next canoe, just behind his, the air noisy with rain and low rumbling thunder in the far distance — was his high-pitched *Please, Miss. Please just listen.*

Clementine was disagreeing of course.

When the camp cook got sick in late May and canceled for the summer, William called his uncle, for whom Clementine had cooked since she was a teenager. Without thinking of the implications, at least not consciously considering them, he asked could Clementine have six weeks off her job to join the camp staff. And Irving agreed.

No, William, Clementine had said. *Under no circumstances am I coming to the northern wilderness of Wisconsin to spend a summer as cook for undiscriminating white boys.*

William had just hung up the phone when she called back.

Unless I can bring Roosevelt.

When William's mother died shortly after he had arrived at his uncle's house in January 1930, he did not know what to do with the overwhelming sadness. He spent the days working construction at an office building on Dupont Circle and evenings in the kitchen, where Clementine was cooking — roasts and stews for dinner, pudding and rich fruit pies — floating around the kitchen like a dancer — high-bottomed, long-legged, small breasts, straight back and strong arms whipping cream, rolling dough for the pie crust, mixing muffins light as air.

Flour whisked with the juices from the roast on the stove — bottles with vinegar on the counter and canisters with sugar and flour, butter softening in a crock, yellow cream, shaved chocolate, the smells so rich and warm he fell into them as if they had materialized with actual shape. Clementine left at nine after the dishes were done, her skin glistening with sweat. She took off the bandana she wore to cook, shook out her hair, washed her face, and said she'd see him in the morning.

Mr. William, she called him.

"Don't call me Mr.," he said. "Just William. Call me by my name."

He called her Clem.

"So, I'm twenty-four," he said.

"Hmmm."

"Well?" he asked. "How old are you?"

"I'm old enough to cook your dinner," she said.

She came early in the morning to make biscuits for breakfast — there were eight of them living at his uncle's house: his uncle's children, his sister, and Clem's mother, who was the "live in" maid. William often got up on those days to be there when Clementine was making the biscuits, cutting in the butter, rolling out the dough, making the round shapes with a cookie cutter. His fantasy — he'd imagine it at night before he went to sleep — was that she take the cookie sheet of golden hot biscuits out of the oven, open a biscuit, slip in a pad of soft butter and pop it in his mouth.

When William got word from his uncle Irving, who got word from a woman in their village, that the Nazis were a threat to the Jews in Lithuania, he finally told Josie that he was Jewish.

"I said I was Catholic so your parents

120

would permit me to marry you," he told her. "I don't intend for them to know anything else, but you are my wife whom I adore and you should know."

He thought at that time, early in their marriage, she was flattered, even pleased that he had lied to win her as his wife. Besides, she couldn't argue. Her parents were quietly enraged at her decision to marry him, which was really not a decision at all but an inevitability.

Josie was a virgin. At the beginning, there was about her body a kind of sexual desperation that delighted him.

Later when she fell into a depression, he blamed himself.

The very fact of who he was and where he had been born.

He grew up in a small village outside the old city of Vilnius, Lithuania. His father was a doctor, and his mother raised her three boys with affection and lack of judgment — he didn't realize until he left home how rare that was — but theirs was, by whatever terms a family life can be assessed, a happy home in a small village of mostly Jews. They were religious and though he chafed against the do's and don'ts — what sometimes seemed the foolishness of religion, any religion — the shape it gave their lives, the repetition of their days, felt rich and necessary.

He left at his father's insistence. His older brothers had gone to school in England, where they had another uncle, and William came to America because, as his father warned him, his quick temper and impetuous nature might be better suited to a New World country than to one in the Old World. William didn't know what that meant, if anything, but he knew he had a wild streak, so perhaps they considered he'd adapt better to a place where anything was considered possible.

He liked America, or what he knew of it. There was a spirit of fluidity and promise or he never would have directed a boys' camp for rich Protestant boys in northern Wisconsin.

Nor married Josephine Hennings.

But *safety* as his parents had imagined America? Maybe not.

"I don't think of you as Jewish," Josie said when William asked her. "I think of you as my husband."

They were sitting in the living room of their apartment in Chicago, Georgianna sleeping. A rare lovely night as William remembered — winter, windy of course and cold, but they were inside — watching the weather, the lake in the distance, the sliver of moon hanging in their window, lights from the buildings around theirs scattered like stars.

Willliam wanted their conversation to move across the room into the night, to somewhere that softened what it was between them. Or not even between them. Just with Josephine, who was still her parents' daughter first and not his wife. Maybe that was at the heart of her frigidity.

Frigidity?

He *could* still hold her in his arms, but when she felt him rise against her body, she pulled away.

"Are you sorry we married?" William asked, thinking if she could say *Yes, I am sorry,* then they could begin again.

This was all before the baby boy was conceived, when Georgianna was still sleeping in a crib.

And then late May, still chilly in Chicago, they were walking to a café for supper and Josie reached for him, her arm around his waist.

"Let's try tonight," she said leaning over, kissing his coat.

Behind William's canoe, there was a string

123

of three boats, close together. The water was suddenly rough enough to induce caution, so they were sticking close in case of trouble, which, with that kind of current, made the paddling difficult. The last canoe, roped to James' boat, contained supplies. James paddled in the stern of the third canoe, Clementine in the bow.

She must be crazy mad by now, William thought. He had promised that the trip upriver would not be difficult. She could sit in the bottom of the boat, take in the sun and breeze and watch the trees pass by. But her strong arms got her the place in the bow. Certainly Adelaide, sitting in the bottom of the canoe, in the middle, a wisp of a girl who was the camp bookkeeper, was no match for Clem.

They were just coming around a bend in the river, a small turn, barely noticeable, and Roosevelt raised his paddle in the air.

"Tree," he called.

William dipped his paddle in pushing the water away to slow the canoe to a stop.

"A tree's down ahead," he shouted to be heard above the wind.

"Can't go any further," Roosevelt called back.

William had always hoped to have Roosevelt

come to camp when he was old enough. It pleased him now to watch the boy's broad back, the straightness of it as he paddled, the muscles in his arms. But it would not have been possible to bring Roosevelt to Minnie HaHa as a camper, so William was paying him the same stipend he paid the others to work on buildings and grounds. The grounds were grounds, the camp carved out of forest mainly pines, cabins nestled in the trees above the river, and the cabins took keeping up. There were ten boys and a counselor in each one. Metal beds, no bathroom — the bathrooms, real bathrooms with flushing toilets, were in a building near the main hall. No windows in the cabins, just screens and no electricity. The boys had flashlights to go to the latrine. Lights out just after sundown.

Roosevelt would stay on the second floor of the main lodge — two dormitory rooms upstairs, one quite small for two women — Adelaide, and this summer, Clementine.

William had not told Clem where she would be sleeping yet. She was going to have a fit.

William's family had a two-bedroom cabin, primitive, but it did have a bathroom and running water, good since Josie wasn't well and would not be willing to traipse to the latrine. Beyond their cabin was James Willow's very small cabin, which James shared with the mice.

William loved James. He was excellent at his work, particularly with the younger boys, and helpful to William in every way except with Josie.

James had never liked Josephine. Something he never mentioned, but William knew and it gave him pause.

William and Roosevelt pulled their canoe to shore.

"Tie up," William called to the others behind him. "We're going to have to portage way off the path to get around this tree."

He lifted Georgie out of the canoe and set her on the bank, where she stood shivering next to Roosevelt. It was very cold for June, and he wrapped his arms around her, rocking back and forth to warm her up.

Josephine was still in the canoe, her head down, resting on her knees, and William walked in his high boots and rain gear into the water, reaching out his hand, leaning in close. She pulled away.

"Josie," he said, his breath in her face. "Are you doing alright?"

She was not. Either it was too difficult for her to get out of the canoe because of her accumulating weight or she didn't feel well or both.

He reached under her arms to lift her forward so she'd have momentum holding onto the sides of the canoe.

"Don't get close to me with your terrible breath smelling like bad meat," she said.

He lifted her anyway. And she gave in to the strength of his arms and he helped her up and out of the canoe, his arm firm around her waist crossing the shallow water to the bank and turning his head away from hers so she could not smell his breath.

William had never given marriage any thought, not in the sense of considering it something a man and woman work at in the hope of achieving some level of contentment.

But recently he had been thinking about marriage.

His life with Josephine was not going well.

His parents had married the community, his grandparents a half a mile away, their synagogue and market and café a short walk which they often took together, greeting neighbors on the street, chatting back and forth. They were as one at dinners in their own houses, at temple, in conversation — William could go right up the road, house to house, and everyone he knew would be living more or less the same life. He'd sit down at their table as if it were his own.

His was not the kind of temperament who spent time thinking about the things in his life he could not change, although he thought he should be able to change his life with his wife.

Just that spring he had found himself restless and irritated with Josie, a flash of irrational temper lurking just below the surface. A fleeting mental vision of slapping her rosy cheeks, of pushing her down the steps of their apartment building into the avenue, of pouring hot coffee on her hand when he served her breakfast.

He worried about himself. He needed to pay attention.

"Is something bothering you, Josie?"

"Of course," she said pulling herself up the bank holding onto a branch and to him for support. "Of course there is."

"Will you tell me later tonight?" he asked. "When we get to Missing Lake?"

"Perhaps," she said.

The men took the canoes one at a time along the top of the bank, climbing over roots and fallen branches, a bed of sodden pine needles. The women waited, except for Clementine, who joined the men carrying the canoes.

"Is the weather going to be like this for the whole trip?" Roosevelt asked.

"I certainly hope not," William said.

"It's supposed to clear," James said. "But you can never tell if weather along this river is going to last for days or not. It always feels as if it will last for days."

"I hope there'll be no more trees in the river," William said, his back aching from paddling, from the weight of the boats, the bow of the canoe heavy with supplies.

"So William," James said, his hand on William's arm, walking back after they had dropped the supply canoe in the water. "Who is this woman, Clementine?"

"She's an excellent cook who works for my aunt and uncle," William said. "When Patricia dropped out as cook this summer, I asked my uncle if Clementine could have the summer off."

"And Roosevelt?"

"Her son," William said, hearing the tension in his own voice. "I've known him since he was a baby, and I'd always planned to hire him for the camp when he reached eleven just to get him out of the wicked summers in Washington."

"Not a lot of colored people up here," James said.

"No," William agreed, but he was startled by James' remark.

"You should have called me about a cook," James said. "I know a great one in Madison who's out of a job."

It took them a couple of hours in the rain and cold to move the canoes to the other side of the tree, eating jelly sandwiches while they worked.

"Missing Lake tonight?" James asked.

"There's no good place to pitch our tents before that," William said. He sat down on the damp ground with Josie, a tarp beneath them.

"I want to go home," Josie said.

"Chicago?"

"Ann Arbor."

William had been afraid of this.

"We're going to camp first," he said. "Whatever you decide after that, we'll get to camp tomorrow not long after three. It will still be light."

"I want to be certain you *do* understand I'm not staying at camp this summer."

They were sitting down away from the rest of the group lined up on the bank, finishing lunch — everyone but Clementine, seated against a tree trunk away from the bank, her hat, the kind that fireman wear, pulled down over her eyes so she could barely see out.

Trouble, Clementine.

James was sitting down beside her in what William assumed was a gesture of friendship, but he noticed that she did not lift her hat.

All Clementine could see in the space between her hat and the wet ground was James Willow's fisherman boots, green with a black border.

"So you're Clementine," James said.

He reached out and dropped an orange in her lap.

He already knew her name — they'd been introduced that morning.

"So how did you end up coming along on this trip?" he asked. "You're a friend of William's?"

He lit a cigarette.

"Mind?" he asked, brushing the pine needles off his boots. "A Washington acquaintance of his, right? I was his student in high school in Chicago."

She shrugged.

"I cook for his uncle's family," she said. "One of my jobs, but in summer people go away on long vacations."

"I've been to William's apartment," James

said, sensing that might make a difference to her. "You can see the lake from the windows in the living room."

"Nice."

She pulled her hat lower on her brow.

Clementine *would* have liked to see the place where William lived, to see how he was living these many years after he had been with the Groves, in the small bedroom without a closet at the top of the stairs when she had known him better.

She wondered whether he had Oriental rugs from Turkey on the floor in his Chicago apartment and oil paintings of Josephine's family on the wall, a grand piano like the one the Delanos, for whom she was a nanny by day, had in their living room even though nobody played — real china from England, maybe Wedgwood, a complete silver service on the buffet.

Dr. Irving Grove had said it was a lucky break William had met Josie, who was from a family with money. Or if not with money, then certainly upper-class.

Upper-class? Whatever that was. Mrs. Delano was upper-class but not the Groves. The Groves were too intelligent for that. Too educated.

As far as Clementine could tell, being upper-class only held you back in life.

Mrs. Delano had not been to school at all, so who would want to have a serious conversation with her, since likely she had learned nothing more at home where she had been educated than how to fold her husband's underwear and crochet the seats for the chairs in her dining room and smile at men in a flirty, submissive kind of way.

Clementine had been to Spelman College in Georgia and had a Bachelor of Arts degree, which her mother Essie framed and put up above her bed in her own room, where she was a live-in at the Groves.

James Willow was a strange man, Clementine thought. Did he think she would be pleased to have him sitting there beside her? Did he think he was appealing and she would be flattered to find him inching closer — his arm just barely pressing against her side, one leg resting against her outstretched legs hidden in high fisherman's boots?

"William came to this camp as director several years ago," James was saying. "And then he fixed it up — more or less fixed it up. It's primitive but nice. You'll find it nice. And then he hired me maybe in the second summer, and on that first canoe trip headed up the Bone River, it was only me and William. And Josephine in Chicago pregnant with Georgianna,"

James had a wet stick in his hand and was breaking it carefully in tiny pieces, collecting in his lap.

"Just us, and from the start I didn't like Josephine," he said, clasping his hands together, rubbing his knuckles against his chin. His jaw, sharp-boned, was set.

Clementine wrapped her arms around her legs, rested her chin on her knees.

Did she want to know why? went through her mind.

Don't get involved, her mother had told her many times. *White folks' secrets can bring you down.*

"I don't know Josephine," Clementine said. "This is the first time I've met her."

"Josephine wants me fired," James said. "I don't know that for a fact, but it is true and is going to happen sometime, one summer or the next or the next and I love it here and I love William." He put his hands to his face as if to stop himself. "I dislike her."

He had a handkerchief in his back pocket and pulled it out and blew his nose.

"I can't control myself," he said. "I'm terribly sorry."

Clementine took off her hat, shook the rainwater and put it on the back of her head.

"Sometimes that happens." Her voice to her surprise was soft. "We just can't help ourselves."

James got up, ran his fingers through his straight blond hair, a nice-looking man, Clementine thought, not handsome exactly, more of a pretty face than a strong one, but he was appealing. Not the man she had expected him to be.

"I don't know why I blurted out," he said. "I'm not that sort of person."

He didn't finish.

She watched him walk off toward the water, away from the bank where the others were having lunch. She was glad he'd left — the conversation hanging in the air between them. Had he remained sitting next to her, his fists together as if he were about to use them, then what to say?

Clementine had not spoken with Josephine except *Hello* when the trip began, but she would not have recognized the beauty now lost in flesh that William's uncle had described when he came home from their wedding in Ann Arbor.

Even on the open river, the sky above them, a sense of fluid space, of change, Josephine Grove's silence was palpable. Fury is what it felt like to Clementine.

Lucky she'd come on this dreadful trip if for nothing else than to protect Roosevelt from the sense she had of trouble.

135

■ ■ ■ ■

"Tonight," William was saying to Josie as he stood preparing to leave, "when we get to Missing Lake and after the tents are up and we've eaten dinner, let's put Georgianna in the tent with Adelaide and sleep together in the smaller tent."

She didn't reply.

"And then when we get to Minnie HaHa, if you still want to go to Ann Arbor, I'll see that you get there."

"I'll be taking Georgianna with me."

"Of course," William said, a sinking in his stomach.

Clementine had stood up, her hands in the pockets of her rain slicker, and William could sense even at that distance she had her eyes on him, walking in his direction straight-backed, her head high. Haughty.

The first time William had visited Clementine McCrary at her house on the corner of V Street and 14th, it was late February, daylight, a Saturday. He had brought cold meat and beer and leftover corn pudding from his uncle's ice box. Not the last time they shared a meal at her house and talked about their hopes and dreams.

She had left the front door unlocked, and William walked in without knocking, stepping into the living room where Clem was standing at a window, her back to him, watching the steady fall of snow. Her hair up, off her slender neck, a dark green dress, probably silk, narrow at the waist, articulated the length of her body, the strength of her shoulders, and William was stirred by the sight of her.

"Welcome," she said. "I was hoping you'd drop by and make this shabby house of mine a home."

Later, at dinner, the baby sitting under the table banging a frying pan with a wooden spoon while they ate, Clem told him about Roosevelt, how his father had left for Texas as soon as she was pregnant.

Left for good, she said.

The clouds had lifted, the sun had come into view coming on three in the afternoon, a golden sun, the color of a tangerine, richer than orange and soon to begin its drop from the sky in the west, north of the ambling storm clouds. The wind had died down too, and William walked along the bank, lifting the canoes, pushing them back into the river.

"We might make it to Missing Lake before

dark," he called, holding Georgie's hand, his arm tight around Josephine's waist as they headed down the small embankment.

The water was dazzling now, striped with light and color, deep blues and a mossy green, pale yellow across the rippling surface.

Roosevelt was already seated in the bow when William reached the first canoe and lifted Georgie in, Josephine holding tight to his waist for balance.

"William?" Josie's voice in his ear was flat. "I don't like the new cook."

After dinner — late since they had arrived at Missing Lake at dusk — the group dispersed. James to the river. The air was preternaturally still. No stars. A dim trace of crescent moon. Dark except for the remains of the campfire and the shadowy figures of counselors milling about.

By ten, most everyone had gone to bed except James, standing on the bank with his back to the river, his hands folded behind him. In the darkness, he could make out the figure of William standing next to Josephine in front of the tent where they would sleep.

Josephine was sitting in a folding camp chair.

James kept track. He knew that the cook had gone for a walk after dinner, upriver in the direction they were heading, walking along the bank, but he had not seen her come back unless she'd slipped into her tent. That was possible. She was stealthy, that cook. He doubted she could swim.

He had feelings about Clementine — inaccessible to him, but they may only have had to do with his anger at Josephine. Just the fact of Josie in his private life.

Careless to have confessed to the cook his feelings about Josephine.

He thought too much about his emotional life — *unmanly,* his father used to tell him — but he couldn't help himself. He was bothered by Clementine and wished William had not asked her to come to camp and wondered why he had brought her and what was between them if anything, and then he wondered why in the world would he feel jealousy about a colored cook, a servant, even an educated servant.

She had no currency in James' life, so why take an interest?

But he could not help himself.

He liked the son. Roosevelt. He was a quiet boy and hardworking, without an attitude. Handsome. He would be handsome — deep brown with hazel eyes and full lips, high color to his cheeks.

Near midnight and James waited for the chance to speak to William alone, for Josephine to go to sleep or into her tent, inside her sleeping bag. She was a sleeper, Josephine, and wouldn't be waiting up for William to lie down beside her. She didn't have an interest in lying with William or she wouldn't have gotten so heavy. At least that was the way James interpreted her sudden weight gain in the last two years, although he never mentioned anything about it to William.

Clementine was upon him before James even realized she was walking on the bank, swinging her arms along her hips, long arms, slender like the rest of her.

"Hello," she said. "Pretty wet out tonight and the bank's slippery."

"Don't fall in," James said.

"Not my landscape," she said. "I like city dirt."

James had paid enough attention to women to know that this one had an attitude, a sharp tongue, a beauty that eluded him, but he felt her sexuality in the air and guessed that she had more of a sense of James than he would have liked for her to have.

"Heading to bed?"

The question just fell out of his mouth.

"Don't think so," Clementine said, and walked on, stopping by her tent, lifting the flap and checking on Roosevelt.

"Restless," she said to no one in particular.

From the river, James could hear William's voice. He was speaking to Josephine — on and on, and then he said in a voice carried through the air and clear enough for James to hear:

I'll be right back to bed, darling.

Darling!

James didn't move.

William was coming down the hill with a flashlight, headed in his direction, and for a brief and perfect moment, James believed that William was coming down to speak to him.

But in the circle of light spreading into the dark, William turned away, headed toward the tents pitched by the river and stopped next to the shadowy figure of the cook, who was standing beside her tent, one hip up, her hand at her waist.

So Clementine must have been the reason William had come down the hill.

James would wait. Surely William would see him, wonder why he was on the bank looking at the blackness that was the river and would stop to say something to James, even just goodnight.

But William did not.

"I'm sorry the weather has been so wretched, Clem," William said, coming up behind her.

"The weather isn't high on my list of sorrys." Clementine put her hand on a tree, leaning her weight against it. "My own stupidity in coming *is* a sorry."

"The summer will be good," he said. "Especially for Roosevelt. I'm pretty sure of that."

"I doubt I'll get any pleasure at the camp — in fact, my summer looks grim in this godforsaken geography, but I'm here because of Roosevelt so he won't drown in the lake or hear a lot of nonsense from your white boys."

"I know that."

"This wasn't a good idea."

"It might prove to be okay," William said, folding his arms across his chest — he could feel his heart beating against his wrist. "Things will be different once we get to camp."

■ ■ ■ ■

Missing Lake

■ ■ ■ ■

June 17, 2008

FROM THE MEMOIR OF THOMAS DAVIES
(FOR PUBLICATION)

Everyone at the campsite seems to be sleeping — even Oona, who has squiggled into my sleeping bag and is curled up next to me with her thumb in her mouth. I can feel her puppy breath silky on my shoulder.

But I am too excited to sleep.

On this night, sixty-seven years ago, maybe with the same stars, the same shape of moon, a silver crescent cookie in the sky tonight, Josephine Grove was murdered.

Someone had a rope and slipped up beside her in the dark and strangled her.

I know it's creepy, my interest in all this, and I can imagine my father saying, not in his usual gentle tone of voice: *Cut the crap, Thomas.*

But I cannot help it.

It's unlikely but possible that Josephine was killed in her tent and then the killer carried her up the hill. But what a lot of trouble that would have been! According to

Georgie, she was found away from the rest of the travelers, halfway up the hill where we were sitting tonight, so either the killer carried her with a rope already around her neck or she had left the tent, in the middle of the night, maybe to pee, and the killer's plan was in place so he did it there to be efficient.

I'm inclined to believe it *was* my great-grandfather who killed her. Why would he choose to go to prison for the rest of his life and leave his only child to be raised by her grandparents if it wasn't necessary. It could *not* have been Roosevelt, even though that's what my uncle Nicolas has in mind. Uncle Nicolas spends a lot of time thinking about conspiracy ever since he took this job with the almost President Obama, but a seventy-seven-year-old man called Roosevelt whom we'd never heard of until this Christmas — dangerous?

I don't think so.

Besides, Roosevelt is not related to me. If he were the murderer, it would be a less interesting story to tell when I go back to school in the fall.

I have had troubles at school more than I care to mention. Not that people make fun of me because of the way I speak, chopping off my sentences at the end, something that is going to get better when I play Malvolio. Or the fact that I'm the boy I am, which is different.

I'm kind of an untouchable. People are attracted to me in spite of themselves, but that doesn't change my situation.

What would change things is for me to have a better story than I have. I'd tell my story to the kids at school and in no time at all I'd be well known all over the place. Or at least well known at Alice Deal Junior High.

The story that I *do* have is of a boy — smart enough but a poor student, not a bad athlete, a slight speech problem, a boy whose father died of a brain tumor, who lives with his grandmother and mother and a ton of long-term visitors at the Home for the Incurables.

I don't exactly fit in. I don't actually want to fit *in,* but I don't like fitting *out* either.

Before he got sick, my father told me that I needed to find something I could do well. Better than others. Maybe even the best.

Something in athletics is what he suggested since sports is the normal thing for a boy to want to do.

"You're fast," he said. "And you have excellent eye-hand coordination."

My father was not at all athletic. He was a

research physician and worked in a lab —
day and night, sitting on a stool looking at
cells under a microscope, and when he
came home, he read.

Some nights after dinner he pulled the
table back in the dining room, turned on
the music and danced with my mother.
Those were the favorite nights of my childhood. I especially loved it when he had his
arm lightly around her waist, his fingers
spread wide on her back and dipped her so
her long hair brushed the floor.

And then he'd spin her across the room
and, leaning against the yellow wall of our
dining room, he would kiss her on the lips.

I hope I will find a girl with whom to
dance, although I am afraid I have bad
breath.

I told my father that my best sport would
be baseball and that my best position would
be pitcher.

"Good," he said. "Perfect for eye-hand coordination."

It was the year I was nine, and my father
began to come home a little early from the
lab and practice pitching with me in the
grassy field between our apartment building
and the next one. Hours we practiced. In
the beginning it was not what I wanted to
do after school, but I did it because I knew

practicing pitching wasn't something my father wanted to do either and he was doing it for me.

Not that I understood what good it would do me to learn to pitch a baseball, but I got good at it. Better than good.

When my father was in the hospital off and on for a year, I would visit him and he'd want to know about baseball since I had joined a team that I was good enough to join but not good enough to be a star. He'd ask how my pitching was going and I would say it was great although it was not great because I wasn't pitching. I was playing second base, but it pleased him to hear about my pitching — I suppose because he had put so much time into it himself — so I'd go on and on, play by play.

Out at first, I'd say, *two strikeouts, bases loaded, up by one run in the final inning. And I didn't let in another run.*

Then I'd go home actually excited, believing I had told him some of the truth, maybe exaggerated, but it was possible in the future for me to be that good.

He was never going to get to see me play, so I had told him a story of what might be true.

My mother thought it would be a swell idea

if I joined a group of kids who had a dead parent and we got to talk about it together. I didn't want to hurt her feelings because I knew she was trying to help me out, but I couldn't imagine anything worse. So I went once — she dropped me off at the Methodist Church where the group was meeting at seven on a Thursday night, and I went in the front of the building and out the side door to a coffeehouse, where I ordered a latte and a cupcake and read the Personals on the bulletin board near the front of the shop. When my mother came to pick me up, I was sitting on the steps of the church and told her that I had been a failure in the group and would not be going back. Which seemed as fine with her as it had seemed to have me meet with the group in the first place. Go figure!

I wonder what a person who is not a killer — not an ordinary sort of criminal wanting to kill for the sake of killing — would *need* in order to do something that savage. Would he think about it for days, imagine it from the beginning to the end, the way I sometimes imagine with a baseball game, sometimes with a girl.

Or would a fury come over him and, quite out of his control, he'd metamorphose into an animal.

What could have made someone in that company with my great-grandfather so angry that he would *need* to murder Josephine Grove.

Except this little seed I have in my head about marriage. Something my mother tried to tell me right after my father died.

We were at dinner. Dinners after he died were silent. I could hardly bear it. Rosie wouldn't even allow me to turn on music. It hurt her ears, she said.

"So tell me," I asked. "Did you and Dad have a happy marriage?"

"I don't know if there is such a thing as a *happy* marriage," she said. "A marriage is enough to hope for. We had that. And we loved to dance."

She had been a good cook before he died, but nights in that first year before we moved to the Home for the Incurables, where Georgie cooks, Rosie would put a bowl of fruit on the kitchen table, a package of cheese, peanut butter, some bread and milk. Sometimes frozen peas or soup from a can, but mostly that year dinner was cold.

"Your father was a quiet man and I liked that he didn't need to talk a lot," she said. "Now what I miss about him most is talking, so we must have talked often and I didn't realize that until we couldn't any longer."

It seemed particularly sad to me to *miss* something that was already there.

I have never been allowed to use the word *hate,* but I hate Max Rider. Maxmillian, he told me, is his Christian name. Of course it would be Maxmillian!

I looked up the word *hate* in the dictionary just to make sure that I won't *die* if I use it. And it doesn't seem like such a bad word — actually convenient — and the meaning I chose was "intense animosity or dislike," which certainly applies to my feelings about Max Rider, my mother's new boyfriend who she met at the studios where they both paint.

Boyfriend? That is too much for me to comprehend.

In my mind's eye, Maxmillian is sitting in our dining room next to my mother, touching her wrists, which he has no right to touch, his hand on her shoulder, his face moving in as if he is going to kiss her right at the dinner table, kiss her the way I watched my father kiss my mother when they danced.

And that is when I *know* how it feels to hate.

Do I want to kill Max Rider on behalf of my father?

Maybe.

Probably.

I do *want* to kill him. But would I?

I cannot answer that right now.

GEORGIANNA

Georgie leans against the pole of the tent where Rosie and Venus sleep, watching the red embers burn to ash.

No heat.

All the tents are silent — the air rustling in the pine woods, the hard slap of water against the shore.

Only Nicolas pacing by the river, backlit by a full moon, dialing without success the sleepless Obama team on the road to the next event. He walks up the bank and squats next to her, speaking in a stage whisper not to wake his sisters.

"I'm troubled by something you said tonight, Georgie." His hand is folded over the cell phone, his face close enough that she can feel his breath.

"You don't actually believe in some kind of visible resurrection of the past, do you? I think of you as a brilliant anthropologist."

"I'm not a brilliant anthropologist," she

says. "I search for evidence and tell a story about what I see. That's all."

"And what do you expect to see tonight?"

"I don't know what to expect," she says. "Maybe nothing. Maybe only a memory will surface in my mind but so far — nothing."

"Posttraumatic shock."

Nicolas stands, slips his cell phone in his pocket and touches the top of Georgie's head.

"Unlikely there'll be anything to actually see except what's around right now," he says. "But who knows?"

Georgie watches him walk down the bank, at an angle so he won't slip on the muddy ground. He crouches, takes his phone out of his pocket. The screen lights up.

Her backpack is on the ground beside her with the mesh bag where Roosevelt's postcards are wrapped in one of her tee shirts.

The last postcard arrived the Thursday before they left for Wisconsin.

Dear Georgianna,

This is my last note before we meet and I am nervous. I bought new socks today but there's a sweater I saw in the town forty miles south where I occasionally go and I should have gotten it on the spot. It is the blue color of the night sky just before dark when the stars are almost visible. Love, R

Georgie is suddenly homesick.
Homesick — that old familiar visitor, creeps up her body on spider legs like seasickness but worse — *nothing* to alleviate its presence, nothing but itself, an apparition at the end of her childhood bed in the middle of the night.
And why now?
A day away from the place she has always kept in mind as *Home.* Her family gathered around her as if she were dying. The possibility of a discovery. Of evidence that her father was an honorable man.
Or not.
She could be wrong.
When she was young and because her grandparents made their feelings clear to her, Georgie was his silent protector. Never aloud since rarely was her father's name brought up, and if there were questions, mainly ones asked by Georgie, her grandmother's response was *You are certainly too young to understand.*
Nights before she went to sleep, she used to say a prayer to William Grove — promising to protect him even though he was dead. Even now she imagines herself under the

eaves of her tiny room in Ann Arbor, the lights out, the house silent, saying a prayer to save her father.

Save him?

She takes a flashlight and heads up the hill to Thomas' tent.

On her knees, the flashlight beside her so the light illuminating Thomas and Oona is sufficiently diffuse not to wake them, she lifts the flap and leans into the tent.

It is Oona she wants to see.

Oona on her back, her arms stretched in a V over her head, her black curls a rat's nest of tangles from settling herself to sleep at night pulling at her hair.

"Oona *is* you!" Nicolas had said as if Georgie had been folded like a pop-up doll in Oona's frontal lobe to make a second appearance. But it wasn't just her dark hair, or high cheekbones or deep hazel eyes, as if transplanted from a life already lived.

She was fierce.

The light from the flashlight resting at a remove skims Oona's small face — her skin transparent, layered in pastels — pale pink on the cheekbones — a slit of hazel just under the closed eyelids, a single dimple even in sleep.

Malleable as wet clay or biscuit dough or potting soil.

A child is someone specific.

Herself.

But not fierce. Not yet.

Who was *she* at four sleeping in a tent like these tents — not with her parents, but with strangers. Who might she have become if some essential part of her being had not been destroyed by the catastrophe.

If she were to tell Oona that *her* mother is dead, alive at night, gone in the morning — that her father is in prison. What then?

What future history would be set in motion by that news.

Georgie slips her cold hands into the pockets of her shorts and walks cautiously down the hill to her tent. She is thinking she hardly knows herself, all these years in such a hurry to build a home for strangers as if the needs of others could satisfy what has gone missing in herself.

"The Home for the Incurables: EVERY-BODY WELCOME" was the headline for the September 12, 2004, *Washington Post* Style piece about Georgie and her experiment.

From time to time in the months since her seventieth birthday, she writes her own obituary in her head. Never finishing it. Never imagining her funeral.

Georgianna Grove, Anthropologist, Dead at 75 *(or 80 or 84 or 93, depending on her state of mind)*

Dr. Grove, author of HOME: Among the Baos Tribe in Botswana, died on Tuesday —— of ——— after a long illness *(or suddenly)*. A professor of cultural anthropology at George Washington University, she is distinguished as a storyteller rather than as a scholar says Dr. James Angle, head of the Department of Anthropology and a well-known scholar of the indigenous people of Chile.

Professor Grove was born December 17, 1937, in Chicago, Illinois, the only child of William Grove, who *(falsely)* confessed to the murder his wife, Josephine, and died in prison. Georgianna was raised in Ann Arbor, Michigan, by her maternal grandparents. Later a widow of the Vietnam War following the death of her husband, Dr. Charles MacDowell, she leaves three children and three grandchildren.

The obituary as she imagines it is short and impersonal. There is no mention of the Home for the Incurables and no way to identify in her particulars the person she was beyond the fact that she is dead.

■ ■ ■ ■

"Everybody sleeping?" Nicolas asks as Georgie returns to her tent.

"Sound asleep," she says.

"Are you glad you came?" he asks, tucking his phone in the back pocket of his shorts.

"Of course," she says. "It's kind of strange and amazing here."

"It's creepy tonight, Georgie. All these pine trees and the water and the sounds coming from the woods and the smell of mushrooms."

"This is what I thought Missing Lake would be." She readjusts her legs on the rock, resting her chin on her knees. "But it's not exactly what I thought I'd feel."

"Which is how?"

"Worried. The way I feel at first on site in Botswana, as if I'm disturbing a universe that was perfectly happy in the present before I came along to dig up the past. But also . . ." She hesitates. "Gloomy."

Nicolas steps up on the rock next to her, crouching on his heels.

"You! Gloomy?"

Thomas gets out of his sleeping bag, careful

not to wake Oona, and heads down to the tent where Georgie is, making his way across the darkness.

She is sitting on a wide flat rock facing the river, her knees bent, her arms wrapped around her legs.

"Can you talk?" he asks.

Nicolas is on the bank, crouched next to the canoes fiddling with his cell phone.

"What woke you?" Georgie asks. "You were asleep when I checked your tent."

"I was awake," Thomas says, "but lying in the dark I just couldn't sleep thinking about that word you told me."

Reenactment is the word Georgie had used. As if by their presence at Missing Lake this particular night, the murder could happen again just as it had the first time.

But this time it would happen with the family watching.

"Tell me how finding out the truth about your father will erase the trouble that has followed our family since your mother was killed."

"It's called revisionist history just to give it a name," Georgie says. "You discover the truth and all the facts you have lived by readjust to the discovery."

"But you've already lived by those facts forever," Thomas says. "So it's a little late

161

to readjust, right?"

"And wrong."

They have good talks, Georgie and Thomas. She takes him seriously.

"I've been wondering since we got here whether it's really wise to go after the truth," she says. "What might we find that will change the equilibrium of our lives. For the worse."

They sit on the bank. Quiet. The night damp and cold.

"Perhaps it's better not to know."

"I don't like that conclusion," Thomas says. "We've come all this way."

"It is possible that I'll discover something I don't want to know," Georgie says.

"What then?" he asks.

"It depends, doesn't it?" she says. "Being here is different than imagining it."

"That's the trouble," Thomas says. "Being here is worse."

Georgie looks out at the blackness that is the river.

"Do you think we have more trouble in our family than other families?" Thomas asks.

"I don't. We don't," Georgie says. "We have our own kind of troubles. But I've been thinking — marriage has been a problem. My mother was murdered, my father died in his thirties, my husband killed in his thirties, Rosie's husband dead; Nicolas is married again but who knows for how long. And Venus with so many men on her credit card, so many abortions she should be arrested."

When Thomas had asked Venus, who is happy to talk to him about anything — *anything* — she told him that abortion was like scooping out the seeds of a cantaloupe.

A cantaloupe!

Georgie puts her hand on Thomas' shoulder and pushes herself back to her feet.

"Come with me," she says, touching the top of his head, leading the way between the tents, up the hill which is quite steep toward the sign for Missing Lake.

"I know this must seem strange to you, knowing me as a more or less sensible older woman, but tonight I want to sit in the dark at a time the murder might have occurred at the place my mother was discovered."

"I don't think of you as older," Thomas says. "And not really sensible. I mean not unsensible but not exactly sensible either. It isn't the first word to come to my mind about you."

They walk slowly up the hill, her hand on Thomas' shoulder as if the weight of the day has been too much and she is suddenly aging step by step.

Thomas asks if she is okay and she says "Not really" and that worries him.

"You mean *unhinged*?"

"Nothing like that," she says. "I made a plan to come here, certain that it was a good plan, but maybe it's the wrong one. That's all."

She reaches in her pocket for a caramel, wishing she had a cigarette. She hasn't smoked for years, not since high school, but she has a yearning.

"Here we are."

She kneels at the top of the hill beside the sign for Missing Lake.

"You were excited about this trip before we got here," Thomas says.

"Nothing is exactly as it seems," Georgie says.

"I guess," Thomas says.

He is beginning to understand that neither is Georgie exactly as she seems.

What she seems to be is *remarkable*. A superhero straight out of a box of action figures but in street clothes — that is how she appears to people who know her at the Home for the Incurables or her job in the Anthropology Department at George Washington University or at the parties she gives, inviting anyone she knows of any age from

164

anyplace — the furniture pushed back, live music usually by students from the university. Dancing.

She is *flypaper* especially for "lost souls" as Uncle Nicolas says.

But also ordinary people who have jobs and houses and children depend on her spirit of generosity.

The front door to the Home for the Incurables has a sign:

**EVERYBODY WELCOME
PLEASE COME IN**

"The thing we need to remember is that Georgie is an orphan," Rosie said to Thomas after the decision was made to go to Camp Minnie HaHa. "She is an orphan because her father murdered her mother and then he went to jail and died. That is not normal."

Not exactly normal, Thomas agreed.

Sometimes Thomas comes home from school and catches Georgie standing at the large windows in the living room looking out as though she is looking for someone specific who might be coming to the house or planning to move in with them.

But no.

Just looking, Georgie has said.

Maybe she is looking for her parents to appear on the other side of Upton Street and cross Upton between the giant trees the city had planted, up the steps to their house and, seeing the WELCOME sign, walk in.

Once when Thomas came in from school, he found Georgie lying on the living room floor, her legs vertical against the wall, her arms crossed on her chest, and he asked her was anything the matter.

Yes, she said without opening her eyes. *It is.*

She wasn't going to tell him. It was possible she didn't even know, and if she did tell him, there would be nothing he could do about it so he went into the kitchen and opened the cookie jar and didn't ask any more questions.

He has never seen her cry.

They sit at the place Georgie has chosen near the Missing Lake sign and wait.

Thomas is cold and wraps his shoulders in her jacket, buries his chin in his knees.

"What do you think is going to happen?" he asks with apprehension.

"I'm waiting to see," she says.

"For something like a ghost?" he asks.

"Nothing like a ghost. Something like weather."

The wind is picking up. The pines bending — a whine, a high-pitched song — and something else.

For the first time since they left Washington, Thomas wants to go home.

The trip has taken on an aspect of danger. He has never been on a river before except the Chicago River for an architectural tour and the Potomac, and those in daytime.

But never a river in the wilderness beyond a place where human life exists.

Just the galloping force of the Bone River in darkness.

Ever since his father died, Thomas has been afraid.

When he was very young, monsters congregated under his bed at night, as many as ten. He would call out, and his father would come into his room in his undershorts with bare feet, peer under the bed and invite the monsters to come to the kitchen for potato soup and cheese sandwiches and maybe some sausage.

Certainly you monsters must be hungry, he would say to them.

Don't worry, he would tell Thomas, coming back into his room. *The monsters are having a midnight supper in the kitchen. They won't be back.*

Georgie has opened up the maps and is looking at them under her flashlight.

On the map of Missing Lake she has drawn the four tents as described in the *Chicago Tribune* and an X that she has determined is exactly where she is sitting now.

"A map is a simple way to look at the geography of a place to understand the way it is," she is saying. "But that isn't necessarily the way it is."

She moves the map and light over to his lap.

"A map is beautiful and full of a predictable order," she says. "But unrecorded history has occurred on any map of any place and that changes the geography."

Thomas doesn't want to know any more about maps, especially if what he is going to learn includes bad news.

Just in the hours since this trip began, Georgie has actually changed. She isn't the same woman full of high spirits she was when they left on the plane to Chicago.

"Remember Gettysburg?" Georgie is asking. "Maybe three years ago when we went to Gettysburg? You were ten and I told you what had happened there, and you said it could *not* have happened because you didn't see the evidence."

"I don't remember," Thomas says.

But he does. Of course he does.

His father, Dr. Richard Davies, had just been diagnosed with brain cancer. Thomas had been told his father was sick, although he had never been sick before.

Then Thomas was sent by plane to stay with Georgie at the Home for the Incurables while the doctors in Chicago decided what to do.

"I remember that I threw up on the battlefield and we had to go home."

"I think you made yourself throw up so we *could* go home," she says.

She is trying to be lighthearted but this is not a funny trip.

"Do you think something terrible is going to happen here tonight?" Thomas asks.

"Like any minute? Doesn't it seem particularly creepy?"

She wraps her arms around him, rests her chin on his head.

"I'm sorry Thomas. I'm very sorry to frighten you."

He lets Georgie hold him even though what he wants to do is shake himself free of her grip, to run down the hill and wake up his mother and Uncle Nicolas and even Venus, who at least would be able to *read* the alignment of the stars announcing trouble if trouble is in the air.

"What I'm thinking now is this," Georgie points her flashlight at the map. "Here are the tents, and my father's tent with my mother was closest to where we are now sitting. Which means of course that my father could have been the one to kill her since he was so close to the place where her body was discovered. Or she could have left their tent to walk around because she couldn't sleep and someone, my guess is James Willow, because who is to know that James actually discovered her when he could easily have strangled her and dragged her here."

"Not Roosevelt?" Thomas asks.

"Of course not. He was eleven years old," Georgie says. "Don't listen to Uncle Nicolas. He doesn't want to be on this trip."

She's looking now at the larger map of the river, tracing it north, a light pencil line to the top, where the river seems to stop just short of Camp Minnie HaHa.

"The one thing I remember about camp is breakfast. Someone would ring a bell and we'd leave the cabin, all of us, and I'd be holding my mother's hand," she is saying. "I don't have a picture of my mother in my mind, but I have photographs and I do remember her sweet-smelling hand and how I used to kiss it as we walked to breakfast. Except . . ."

She stops, her hand on Thomas' wrist.

"Actually, Thomas, I think I remember nothing about my mother except what I've seen in photographs."

They sit quietly, her arm draped around his shoulders, squeezing his arm a little too tight, and Thomas is beginning to feel he will jump out of his skin, as Georgie likes to say. Then they hear a rustle in the brush behind the tents — not a small disturbance, the kind a beaver or a skunk or badger might create.

But heavier.

"Bear?" Georgie asks.

They listen.

The sound travels through the reeds, moving away. Only the rustle of high grass disappearing into silence except for the wind and the pine trees ringing like chimes above them.

"You think it's a bear?" Thomas asks.

"Whatever it was, it's gone," Georgie says. "I didn't ask the outfitters about bears in these woods."

"Maybe we should go to sleep."

"I can't," Georgie says. "I'm not at all tired."

It is clear to Thomas that they are going to be together on the bank until she is ready to go to bed, if she goes to bed at all, and Thomas will have to stay with her because she wants him to be there.

He feels less trapped when they lie on their backs, side by side, their arms stretched out above them, the high pines barely lit by the slender moon, the current of Bone River slapping water over the bank.

"I don't believe in forgiveness," Georgie says.

Out of the blue she says it, and Thomas' stomach tightens the way it does when he senses an expectation that he will fail to meet.

He is silent, hoping she will change the subject or stop talking or go to sleep, but she isn't in the mood.

He lies very still.

She has turned on her side and is resting her chin in her hand, the way she likes to read in bed at the Home for the Incurables, the lampshade tilted so she can better see.

"Thomas?" she asks, peering over at him. "Are you sleeping?"

He rubs his eyes as if she is waking him up, but she isn't since he hasn't been sleeping.

"I've been wondering whether you were

aware of being angry when your father died?"

"I was angry," Thomas says. "I am still angry."

"At him for leaving?"

"It wasn't his fault," Thomas says. "He would have done anything not to leave us."

"Then who are you angry at?"

"I don't believe in God," Thomas says, "if that's what you're asking me."

"That's not what I'm asking."

There had been no mention of God when his father was ill or dying or even at the funeral in Chicago.

Only of science.

Besides, Thomas would never believe in one god. It only makes sense that there would be many gods like the Greeks believed and the Egyptians and the Romans, all the ancient civilizations. And the gods are half-human and half-god, superheroes who can live ordinary and extraordinary lives at the same time.

His father, Richard Davies, is that kind of god.

Sometime in the middle of the night, they fall asleep.

When Thomas wakes up with a sense of dread, suddenly as though from a dream, which he cannot remember, Georgie is curled on her side facing away from him.

The sky is just beginning to lighten, not even dawn, but he can make out the shape of tents around the crescent of land, a light wind cold on his dew-damp skin, the river splashing against the bank, no sound but the river.

No one else seems to be awake.

He pushes up from the ground, brushes off his shorts, the back of his sweater as far as his hand can reach behind him, checks to see if his glasses are still in his back pocket and heads down the path to his tent.

He wonders if he had dreamt while he was sleeping — if it had been a bear they heard making his lumbering way through the forest and whether Oona curled up in his sleeping bag is awake yet.

At the tent, he holds on to one of the poles for balance, opens the flap that must have closed in the night and peers in the triangle of space. It's too dark to see. He gets down on his hands and knees and crawls to his sleeping bag, running his right hand across the soft quilted material, balancing with his left. He moves his hand and arm from the bottom of the sleeping bag to the top feeling for the body of a little girl.

He does it twice, reaching more slowly

the second time, feeling for a shape in the sleeping bag, a small bottom, the solid bones of a child's skull.

But the sleeping bag is empty.

Completely empty.

He falls across it on his stomach, banging his forehead on the hard ground over and over and over and over and over.

Oona is gone.

■ ■ ■ ■

Missing Lake

■ ■ ■ ■

June 17, 1941

WILLIAM

William returned to his tent, angling up the hill, his ankle twisting on the roots of so many pines crowding the periphery of open land, their roots curling across the landscape.

The damp air was pungent with the smell of mushrooms.

Josie was gone.

No longer in the folding chair where he had left her. A flashlight, the light pointing into the sky, lay where she had been sitting.

The blood rushed to his head.

When he had seen Clementine leaning against a tree next to her tent, he had gone down the hill. He needed to speak with her.

Back in just a minute, he'd said to Josephine.

Now he stared through the darkness beyond the tents, into the forest, suspecting Josie might have gone to the edge of the woods to pee.

Fastidious Josephine.

But why wouldn't she have taken the flashlight?

Or perhaps she had walked down to the tents pitched closer to the water to check on Georgianna, although he was surprised she had been able to get up from the low folding chair without his help.

He stood next to their tent the way he often stood, his arms folded across his chest, his back straight, surveying the river. Two tents, side by side, swallowed the dark — one with Georgianna, the second, closer to the water, with Roosevelt.

Where Clementine would sleep should she ever decide to go to bed.

He doubted Clem was afraid in this geography, the way another woman might be. But she was angry and didn't hide the heat of her anger in a soft cushion of innuendo the way Josephine was inclined to do. She spoke her mind. William liked that about her.

When he had called Clem about camp for Roosevelt that summer, they hadn't seen each other for several years. First Georgianna was born in the icy December of 1937. Then the stillborn boy in the fall of 1940 and Josephine's steady retreat.

The long absence from Clementine followed years of visits to his uncle for a weekend every June after school let out, sometimes for New Year's or before school started up after the holiday. Never with Josie, who went home to Ann Arbor. On those visits, he only saw Clem in the kitchen of his uncle's house, where he sat at the long table watching her cook. She didn't linger after work. But he would take Roosevelt out to Rock Creek Park to skip stones in the creek and hike the hills, or downtown to walk the mall or canoeing on the Potomac. During occasional phone calls with his uncle, usually for news from Lithuania, he would ask Irving about Clementine as if in passing.

The campground was eerie with scattered silence. River sounds, a breeze over the wet leaves and low brush. And then what sounded like a soft hum in the distance by the water, coming from one of the tents.

Voices?

He could not be sure.

Earlier in the evening when William caught sight of Clementine, he and Josie had been arguing about food. Whether the new cook would make the fresh peach pies the former cook had made for Sunday supper — *"or just fried chicken and mashed potatoes and ice cream."*

"You're going to be in Ann Arbor, Josie, so what does it matter whether she makes peach pies."

"Just wondering, that's all," Josie said. "The new cook is from the South, where all they eat is fried food or so I understand. And that's not good for these boys."

"I used to eat her meals at my uncle's house," William said. "They were delicious. And seldom fried."

"Then I'll miss these delicious meals since, as you have pointed out, I'll be in Ann Arbor. A loss," Josie said, her voice low in her throat, emanating gloom. "And there she is now. The cook. Almost midnight and she's still awake."

William looked down the hill toward the water following his wife's line of vision, and there was Clem leaning against a tree, her back arched, her head resting on the trunk.

Something about the strength and boldness of her pose. Her blackness against the dark night, her body outlined black on black. He got up and headed down the hill.

"I'll be right back," he called to Josie. "I need to warn Clementine about the river."

"What about the river?" Josie had asked.

But William had headed down the hill as if he hadn't heard her.

He did not linger, did not wish to cause

182

himself more trouble than he already had. Gone just long enough for Josie to disappear.

Squinting to make out the tents in the near distance, walking close to the line of trees, he was overtaken by thoughts of home — deep in his stomach, spreading with a weight greater than his body weight.

Tonight would be tomorrow in Lithuania. The Nazis could be arriving now in his village outside of Vilnius, gathering the Jews, all the Jews in the village of Jews — executing the ones who would not follow orders. His own father would likely resist — the village physician, the caretaker of his people. It was in his father's temperament to quietly stand his ground. He would not likely be collected like the others, the women and children, the more compliant or fearful men, rounded up, off to wherever they were taken. Hard labor. Worse.

William had spoken to his uncle Irving about home the week before he left Chicago for Minnie HaHa.

"There is nothing to be done," Irving had said, resigned, but not without a thin skein of hope, which was a kindness that William understood for what it was.

"Only right to tell you what I suspect."

183

All William knew was what his uncle told him. He didn't ask questions because he didn't want to know any more. He didn't think about home often — and if he did, it was in terms of his dead mother, who wouldn't have to suffer what Irving referred to as *the inevitable.*

He had a vision of his mother in the kitchen shortly before he left for the United States. When he thought of her, she was singing as she seared the meat for lunch, chopped the vegetables, lay out the cutlery for the kitchen table, singing in spite of the encroaching dangers, in spite of her youngest son leaving for America the Beautiful, as she bravely called it.

She had her own kind of beauty, his mother. Not physical, but a beauty inside out, and he liked to think of her singing and cooking, liked to think that with her death he had assumed a part of her spirit.

At the beginning of June just after school let out, a letter arrived from Josie's mother, who seldom wrote. William took it from the mailbox and left it on the dining room table with the rest of the mail. Days later, he found it in the trash. Pale pink stationery torn into pieces, the pieces too small to put together, too small to read although he tried.

"From your mother?" he asked, stating

the obvious, the wide swooping script of privilege on the torn paper.

"It is," Josie had replied.

"And you tore it up?"

"I did," she said. "My mother . . ." she began, dropping the rest of the sentence, but William knew what it was on her mind to say.

They were at breakfast in the kitchen of their Chicago apartment, a pale early summer sun over the lake. Josie, her chin resting in her fist, looking out the window.

"You lied to my parents, William."

"Otherwise you *could not* have married me. We have spoken about that."

"I should not have married you. We are made from different cloth."

"Cloth? Because I'm Jewish?"

"Because you lied."

A kind of desperation overtook him as he headed down the hill toward the river. He tried to take in air enough to settle his nerves, to slow the rapid beating of his heart, but there was not enough air.

He needed to be with Josie.

Tonight.

For weeks, months, he had felt an accumulating rage, bouts of quick, explosive temper, his jaw locked, his teeth grinding even when he was awake.

It had been more than a year since he had been with Josephine.

Then one afternoon when the regular camp cook, a woman from Chicago, called to say she could not work the coming summer, William instinctively picked up the phone and dialed his uncle for permission to ask Clementine.

His uncle agreed it would be a good break for Roosevelt, and William called her — the first time in months that they'd spoken. Certainly he knew it was likely a bad decision as soon as Clem reluctantly agreed to come.

For the sake of Roosevelt, she said.

By habit or inclination William tended to move forward in his life, confident of his instincts day to day. Not unreflective, but reactive. Drifting as he had through a childhood that seemed to promise a predictable future, he left for America with a sense of adventure. Not fear of what might happen in his absence to the people he loved and left behind. Nothing had happened when he lived in the village where he grew up, only whispers among the dependable grown-ups to which he paid little attention any more than to the ordinariness of their quotidian life.

At his uncle's house, especially after the news of his mother's death, Clementine McCrary became a touchstone — her generosity of spirit, her beauty and certainty and strength. The kitchen had been the sacred place of his childhood, watching his mother cook, and in America, with Clem, it became again the center of his days. What he remembered at night, often sleepless and alone in the dark, was Clem's constancy in an unpredictable new life.

"Why can't we be real friends?" he had asked her once, although it should have been perfectly clear even to an immigrant from Eastern Europe living in segregated Washington, D.C. "Just do things together. Normal things."

"We are friends."

"But why should a matter of color make such a difference?"

"All the difference," she had said.

William left for graduate school in Michigan.

And married Josephine, fathered Georgianna — etcetera, etcetera, as he said to his uncle. A regular American life infused as if by a slow drip of poison in his veins, befuddling his brain.

That was how he felt this night on the Bone River as the Nazis were surely by now entering his village.

William needed something to happen with Josie this night. He *wanted* to make that clear to himself.

His Wife.

The Camp Director's wife. The wife of a Doctorate in Physics from the University of Michigan for what that was worth.

The wife of a Jew. The father of her child.

Not a Jew, this child.

He was negotiating the rocks and roots on the hill that led down to the river when there was a shout — more like a crow's call, a gravelly shriek.

For chrissake — NO!

Straining to look in the direction of the tent, William could make out two figures — the tall, lean, straight-as-a-pole body of Clementine and the smaller, rounder, familiar shape of his wife.

He took a step to the right into the darkness, out of the moon's reach.

"William?" James put his hand on William's arm, his voice a whisper.

"I didn't even see you," William said.

"Trouble," James said.

"I don't know what's going on," William said.

"What you heard just now was the cook."

"I could tell it was the cook," William said. "I know her voice."

They stood side by side, off to the right where the woods took over the landscape — their shoulders touched, their lanky figures melted into the trees. James, fair-skinned, the taller and thinner of the two. William — five feet ten — rugged, slender and fit. Dark-skinned by birth and years in the out-of-doors.

"Did you hear the argument?"

"I did," James said. "I was just by the river when Josephine pounced."

"Pounced?" William gave a small laugh. "Josie?"

"Josie, yes. She said to the cook in a voice loud enough for me to hear her clearly, *We've never had Negroes at this camp.*"

William felt his blood drain.

"That's not like Josie, James. She is difficult, but she isn't cruel."

"Maybe jealous?"

"I'm not sure that Josie has enough interest in *me* to be jealous."

"It was a mistake, you know it was a mistake, William, to ask his cook to join the camp this summer."

189

"Possibly."

"So why did you ask her?"

"She's an excellent cook," William said, "and I wanted Roosevelt to have a healthy summer. Washington is wretched in the heat."

James shrugged.

"Also," William said softly. "She was kind to me when my mother died."

Below on the riverbank where the women had been arguing, Josie had moved out of view.

"Is it possible that you have more than a professional interest in the cook?" James asked.

"It is not possible."

"Well . . . it's fraught and we aren't even at camp yet."

"What has been going on?"

"This is what I know," James began in a stage whisper. "What I heard standing just about where we are right now. Nervous as a cat, something about the weather and the wind. And here comes Josie down the hill, heading straight for the cook."

He settled just slightly against William.

"The cook was leaning on the tree, and Josie had stopped just there by the tent where the cook's son is sleeping. *Good eve-*

190

ning, the cook said, and Josie replied — quite loud because I was over here in the woods where we are now and I heard each word in spite of the wind." James spoke quickly. "What she said stopped me in my tracks."

"What did she say?"

"She said, *I want to know if you are here because you have an interest in my husband, William Grove, the director of this camp. That is what I want to know.*"

William leaned his head back against the pine branches.

"And that's when the cook said *For chrissake, NO!* So loud that you could hear her up the hill," James said.

"That does not sound like Josephine."

"Maybe not, but that is what she said."

"She'd be ashamed to reveal herself in such a manner to . . ."

"To a Negro?"

"That is *not* what I was going to say, James."

"So you must have heard what the new cook said in response."

"I heard *For chrissake, NO.*"

"And then she said —" James continued.

"Her name is Clementine," William said. "You know that, so call her by her name."

"She said, *I am a cook in the home of his*

191

uncle, Dr. Irving Grove, and do not occupy the same world as William Grove."

"That's the whole conversation?" William asked.

"It was just a conversation," James said. "Not a calamity or I wouldn't have told you. A little cat fight that I thought would be of interest to you."

William pulled up his trousers, tightening the belt. He kicked one muddy boot against the other, scanning the darkness.

"Did you notice where Josie went?" he asked.

"Along the bank just a moment ago," James said.

"She's not a swimmer."

"She's not going to fall in the river," James said. "She's too cautious for that, as you would say yourself."

"Upset, anything can happen," William said.

"I see someone now moving in the woods."

"Where?"

"Just there, on the bank above the river."

A small round figure emerged from the trees heading toward the tents.

"I'm sorry." James' hand was gentle on William's arm. "I know that things are not going well at home."

"They aren't." William brushed by James' shoulder as he turned.

He was suddenly concerned about James. Whether they were friends or not, whether their friendship was in the balance.

Who to trust and who not? Or was *trust* even a word worth considering.

Was James actually pleased to see William in a trouble spot?

Fair-haired James with his perfect bones, his fine Anglo-Saxon skin and slim figure.

Did he wish William well? Or did he not.

William had met James when he was a student in a junior-year class in European history and philosophy. His best student — an odd boy who spoke a kind of lyrical prose in a soft, insistent voice reminiscent of the boys in his classes in Lithuania.

A mannered acquiescence about James. And something else William couldn't identify.

"Mr. Grove," James would say in class, "It has come to my attention —" Always that: "It has come to my attention . . . ," as if James was the one student at Boys' Latin High School who might be capable of understanding the significance of a historical event.

William would find himself almost by accident falling into James' strange web of worship and rejection as if the one led almost immediately to the other.

"You're a simple man, William," James had once said to him.

"Simple?"

"Not in a bad way," James said. "Quite the contrary. You don't make a mountain out of a molehill, the American expression for *reasonable.*"

They had long talks, especially in the years they traveled together, just the two of them. William especially liked the talks about history, but he didn't care for the long, personal conversations turning William inside out as if James were engaged in a dissection in the biology laboratory, as if he wished to know William way beyond William's own interest in himself.

But lately, since last summer, William had become uncomfortable with James.

A wariness, as though there were something James wanted from him more than the friendship they had had as teacher and student.

A friendship that had been a matter of fact for William.

But maybe not.

When he got back to the tent at the top of the hill, Josie was in her chair, the flashlight in her lap and turned off.

"You followed me?" she said.

"I didn't follow you," William said. "When I came back up from warning Clementine about the river, I assumed you'd gone to the woods to relieve yourself."

He dropped down beside her.

"But you had left."

"I went down the hill to speak to the cook."

"I know that now."

"She has an attitude." Josie looked up at him. "Wouldn't you agree she has an attitude?"

"Possibly." He could not deny that about Clem. "Did you check on Georgianna?"

"She's sleeping."

"So she's okay."

"I said she is sleeping."

Josie turned on the flashlight, swirling it in a circle, nervously swirling round and round, shining it into the sky, light zigzagging crazily across the horizon.

Stop! was on the edge of William's tongue as he stood up from the camp chair, but he refrained.

He ducked inside the tent, sat on his sleeping bag, untied his boots and put them behind his pack, shook out the double sleeping bag and crouched in the darkness, collecting himself, watching the back of Josephine, her hair pinned up off her neck, thinking what to say, what possibly was there to say to change the direction of the air between them.

"William?" Josie was sitting directly in front of him, facing the river.

He didn't stand and she didn't turn around to face him.

"James told me earlier that the Nazis were taking over Lithuania in the next few days."

"So I understand."

"Your uncle told you?"

"He did."

"Is that what's been on your mind making you so cruel?"

"I didn't know I had been cruel."

"You seem crazed, like a trapped animal. I don't feel safe."

"I am not conscious of being an animal, Josie."

"You are too tightly wired, William," his mother would say to him. "Stand straight, take six deep breaths one after the other and breathe out slowly."

William would follow her instructions.

She was his mother and they were in Lithuania and he was young.

He had only once gotten into serious

fisticuffs in school, a fight he lost, with a bloody nose and a broken hand. But the boys in school were wary of him. He was known to have a temper.

Even now, the broken hand, poorly set in the clinic, was sensitive to weather.

"I'm ready for bed, Josie," he said quietly, a whisper of seduction in his voice which he intended as much for himself as for Josephine.

He took off his trousers, folded them on top of his boots, ran his hand over his stomach. Taut — the belly from winter flattened.

Josie reached out her hand, unable to stand from a low chair without his help. There was pain in her face.

"Does something hurt?" he asked.

"Nothing hurts," she said.

He climbed into the sleeping bag, sitting up, still in his heavy sweater, watching while Josie sorted through her belongings for a gown, undid her hair so it fell to her shoulders, her face still lovely in repose. She found the gown, changed her mind, stuffed it back in the pack and climbed in next to him fully clothed.

"Too cold?" he asked.

"Too cold?"

She pushed the top of the sleeping bag

into a facsimile of a pillow and lay down on her back.

"Sleeping in your clothes."

The sleeping bag was pulled up to her thighs, her arms across her stomach and William lay next to her, pushing down so they were side by side.

He reached over and took her hand in his. Gently. She did not resist.

Lying on his back, his jacket folded and under his head, he watched the slow rise and fall of her belly. The way a tendril of her curly hair fell across her cheek, her cheek flushed.

He lifted her hand across his groin and lay it on his cock.

She was still and quiet, her breath soundless — her eyes closed, a light flutter of eyelash, a tightening of her lips.

"Josie?"

"Yes."

In the distance, a rumble of weather, the high screech of a hawk settling to quiet, a light wind.

"Do I disgust you?" he asked, turning off the kerosene lamp.

Josie turned her head away, looking into darkness — her hand lifeless against him.

Missing Lake

■ ■ ■ ■

June 18, 2008

GEORGIANNA

A muddy dawn spreads through the tent, and there in the place where Oona had been is Freddy, the scruffy pink pig. Thomas waits, his breath trapped in his throat.

Just up the hill, Georgie is stretched out on top of her sleeping bag, her arms extended above her head, her hands open, palms up. Her eyes are closed, but she is not asleep. In fact, quite awake, lightheaded thinking with actual relief that they have made it through the night. No visitations. No terrible storms galloping down the Bone River. Morning, and soon the sun would break through.

Today, Roosevelt.

She sits up, stretches, spreading her fingers in the chilly air.

Ahead, Thomas' back is in her line of sight.

Strange.

He is just sitting there on his haunches.

She rolls her sleeping bag, ready to leave for Minnie HaHa, and comes up quietly behind him.

"Are you okay?" she asks, kneeling down beside him.

He is not okay. He can't catch his breath to speak, his hands are fisted. A sound like a hum in his throat.

"Oona."

His voice is not his own.

Georgie looks into the tent at the empty sleeping bag where Oona had been.

"Gone?"

Thomas nods.

Georgie moves slowly, stops to gather her wits, settle her racing heart.

"I knew something would happen to Oona on this trip," he says,

"Maybe she climbed into the sleeping bag with Nicolas."

Georgie's mind rushes to solutions.

"Or maybe she's with Rosie."

"If she woke up in the middle of the night, she would have come up the hill to find me," Thomas says. "Not Nicolas or Rosie and *not* Jesse."

He takes Georgie's hand and she pulls him to his feet.

"I think she drowned."

"No, Thomas. She did not drown. She's a

careful girl and wouldn't go to the water in the dark."

"She would do that," he says. "I know her very well."

"We'll check," Georgie says. "We'll check the tents to see if she is there. Then check the river and the path along the bank."

They walk down the hill, Thomas leaning against Georgie, a dead weight at one hundred pounds.

"Everything will be okay, won't it, Georgie?" he asks. "You think that, don't you?"

Georgie lifts the flap of Nicolas' tent.

Nicolas is on his back, the cell phone beside his head. Jesse lying on his side in his sleeping bag, his eyes open.

"Nicolas?" Georgie asks.

"He's awake," Jesse says. "He snores when he's asleep."

"I was wondering is Oona here?" Georgie asks as though it is the most casual of questions.

Though it is clear that Oona is not.

Jesse shakes his head.

"Oona?" Nicolas sits up and grabs his phone. "She was sleeping with *you,* Thomas."

"She wasn't sleeping with me any longer." His voice is barely audible.

"But she was, isn't that right. She was

sleeping with you all night for chrissake."

"Not all night," Georgie says quietly.

Since she can remember, she has been able to turn the nerves in her body on *low,* necessary in the fieldwork she does in Africa.

"Last night, Thomas and I were talking just up the hill and Oona was sleeping in the tent below us so we could see her. We could see very well even in the dark."

Nicolas pulls up his pants and zips them.

"If you could see, then you should have seen her leave the tent, isn't that right?" His voice is trembling. He picks up a sweater from the ground and pulls it over his head.

"I didn't sleep all night. Only some of the night," Thomas says. "I didn't really sleep, not hard, but I was up there . . ."

He points to the hill where most of the night he had been talking to Georgie.

"I was up there with Georgie and we could see everything."

"What the fuck!" Nicolas heads up the hill, Thomas and Georgie just behind him as he lunges into the tent where Oona had been.

"Freddy's here," he says, coming out with the pink pig.

"Right here," he says, swinging the pig.

"Oona would never leave Freddy behind."

He shakes his fists in the air. "You guys were supposed to be in charge of my daughter, *Got it, Thomas?* — you were going to be sleeping next to her and she fucking trusted you with everything."

Nicolas draws back, fists his hands and in an awkward movement, almost like a dance, he hits his head with his own fists.

Blows to his cheekbones and his skull, a long high wail, the sound of an injured animal rising out of him.

Venus is coming from the tent where she has been sleeping.

"What is happening?" She starts up the hill. "Nicolas!"

"We don't know," Georgie says.

"We do know," Nicolas says. "We know that Oona is gone," he calls out in a loud voice. "My daughter disappeared in the middle of the night in this godforsaken forest."

"Gone?"

"Thomas was supposed to be sleeping with her," Nicolas says, bending at the waist as if his stomach is cramping.

"And he didn't sleep with her. He left her alone. *Alone,* and she's four years old."

"This is not Thomas' fault," Georgie says under her breath.

"It *is* my fault," Thomas says quietly.

"It is *my* fault," Georgie says.

"It *is* your fault, Georgie, for bringing us on this trip. And so what! So fucking what if we find out who it was that killed your mother. Or why. Or what difference your mother should make to any of us. Or your father."

A kind of growling sound from deep in Nicolas' body as though something inside has erupted and shatters the air.

A sound like the commotion of birds, and he falls to his knees, his forehead on the ground, his arms straight out by his head. Sobbing.

"Nothing has happened yet, Nicolas," Georgie says, although he cannot hear her. "We need to think. We need to be clear headed and think. What to do next? What to do."

"Maybe she sleepwalked," Thomas says quietly. "I know someone at school who sleepwalked in the middle of the night straight down Wisconsin Avenue to the Cathedral."

"I don't know about sleepwalking," Georgie says, moving past the tent where Oona had been, onto what appears to be an actual path beyond the campsite.

"What happened?" Rosie calls.

And then Jesse.

Certainly it is Jesse who is crying.

She must keep calm, she tells herself as she comes to the boundary of land and forest. Settle her mind before it closes in on itself, expand her brain so its narrow roads open to possibility.

So she can think.

But her heart is pounding against her breastbone as if it might fly out of her chest.

If Oona woke in the middle of the night and didn't know where she was or couldn't find anyone or couldn't see in the dark, she would cry out.

Certainly she would call or scream or wail that terrifying breathless sound she made when she was hurt.

But nothing.

If she left the tent, by choice and on her own, in secret, then certainly she would have taken Freddy with her.

Someone must have taken her out of the tent. Someone who knew that she was there. A person hiding in the woods behind their encampment had located the tent where Oona was sleeping and gone after her.

Perhaps it was the bear. The one they had heard last night thumping in the woods.

But not a bear. Not possibly a bear.

She senses Thomas coming up the path behind her like a cat, light on his feet, graceful for a tall, quick-growing boy.

She doesn't turn around, keeping her eyes ahead. Checking the floor of the wet, black path for information. When Thomas does catch up with her, she will tell him to go back to camp. She needs to be alone.

She *will* tell him that.

She must have silence to consider the possibilities. To act. Not randomly, the way her mind is scattering in bits, but with intention.

"This is the end of our family," Thomas says, catching up with her.

"It is not the end of our family," she says. "Nothing has happened. Nothing conclusive."

"How can you know?" Thomas leans against her.

"I can't *know,* but I can believe we will find her."

"Will she be alive?"

"Of course she will be alive."

There is not enough oxygen in the dawn air, and it doesn't help to have Thomas beside her, leaning into her shoulder, taking up the little air that's left.

It never occurred to her when she was planning this trip that they would be out of touch with the world. She did not think to ask and didn't know until they arrived at the lodge, although Roosevelt had told her there was no cell service at camp. Only a land line.

But no cell phone service anywhere?

"Where are we going?" Thomas asks

"We'll search the campsite, and if we don't find her, then the rest of you need to go on to Minnie HaHa, where Roosevelt will be able to help. He has a telephone and can call the police."

"That man at the lodge said the river police patrolled at eight in the morning every day."

"I heard him say that, but it's only five-thirty in the morning now," Georgie says.

"What would you do if something terrible happened in the village in Botswana? You didn't have communication there."

"There I'm in a community of people who know the land and each other," she says. "It's not the same. Here it is only us in a place we do not know."

"Really scary."

"Or maybe not," Georgie says.

She is searching for a plan.

They *could* all paddle to Minnie HaHa, but that would take hours, two at least. Hours lost for looking.

Or they could split up. The rest of her family paddle to camp and Georgie remain.

Walk the pine needle path, although it may only lead in a circle or come to an end.

Or the path could end at the town of Missing Lake if such a place exists.

"I'm sure she could have drowned," Thomas says.

"She didn't drown."

"But she could have," Thomas says. "Anything could have happened. She could be dead."

"No, Thomas, she could not."

She takes his hand.

"It is a bad idea to think the worst," she says. "So don't."

Georgie has a way of allowing a place to wash over her like weather. When she arrives, even to be with the Baos in Botswana, where she has been many times, it is always as a stranger. She waits for the place itself to infuse her blood.

What she needs now is footing. A sense of solid ground. Then some combination of what she actually sees and her imagination will deliver clues.

"I am looking for evidence," she says to Thomas, keeping pace.

"Like what?"

"I'm going back to ask Nicolas to take the canoes to Minnie HaHa. There he can get help from Roosevelt and I will look for Oona."

"I'll be able to look with you, won't I, Georgie?"

"You can come Thomas," she says, walking into the clearing above the river, "but as a ghost."

Nicolas is calling her name — but what she hears is lost in an endless cry . . . his voice unnaturally high and cracking. She turns toward the river, silver light on the water, the land black, but she can see Nicolas by her tent where she did not sleep — face-down, his fists pounding the ground.

She walks down the hill with care, the ground muddy, slippery with dew, a sudden neuropathy in her feet from nerves or cold.

Slipping down beside him, her hands rest on her thighs — she leans in speaking quietly in his ear, speaking with a kind of certainty, the way she had spoken to him when he was a child.

"I need you to take a canoe with Rosie and Jesse and paddle to camp Minnie HaHa," she says. "It is just before six in the morning and we have no cell phone service. No possibility of reaching *help* until the police begin their patrol on the Bone River two hours from now."

She sits back on her haunches, lets her hand slip gently on the small of Nicolas' back.

"You will be there in two hours and it won't even be eight o'clock. Roosevelt can call the police. He will know what to do."

Nicolas has pushed himself up to a sitting position, his face muddy with tears and dirt, his eyes deep black pools of fear.

"She disappeared right here," he says. *"Here!"* He bangs the ground, a low roar in his throat. "I don't want to leave right *here* where I am this minute and move further and further away from where Oona might be." He catches his breath. "I won't leave."

"I will stay, Nicolas," Georgie says. "The woods are too dense to enter, so I'll walk the path behind the campsite, maybe into the town of Missing Lake. Maybe not. But I'll be here when the police boats come. It is the most sensible thing to do."

"This has nothing to do with sensible," he says.

But he is standing now, brushing the dirt off his pants.

"Rosie?"

Rosie is putting the paddles in the canoe.

"I'm checking the woods, just the ones in this cove, and then we'll leave," Nicolas says.

His voice is subdued but steady.

"We can make it to Minnie HaHa before the police cruise the river at the campsite this morning."

Georgie stands, taking the map of the campsite from Thomas.

There is a road that more or less follows the shape of the river. Not close to the water but the road curves running by what seems to be a town, marked on the map with a tiny brown circle. Not even a name given to the brown circle.

In the distance Nicolas is heading into the forest, his arms raised in surrender above his head as he tries to angle through the trees.

An eerie sound pierces the air like the sound of a loon.

"Nicolas?" Thomas asks.

Georgie nods.

"What are we going to do?" Thomas asks. "Now? Just wait? It's driving me crazy just standing around like this."

"We're going to wait for Nicolas to come back. The woods are so overgrown I doubt he will get far. Then he will leave for Minnie HaHa with the rest and we'll search along the path for Oona."

They stand, silently watching the Bone River accumulate a golden color as the sun rises from underneath the world.

"No sign of Oona in the woods," Nicolas says, "but I'm too nervous to search like that."

There is nothing else to say.

Georgie wants Nicolas to leave. She will be better with him gone.

"So now we're off to Camp Minnie Haha," Nicolas says. "Maybe Roosevelt will know something. Maybe *he* took Oona."

"Why would *he* take Oona?" Thomas asks.

"Because she's a little girl and he's an old man and he *wanted* to take her."

"Nicolas!" Georgie says.

"Well . . ." he shrugs, "I'm not stupid. Did he know that Oona was coming on this trip?"

"He knew all of you were coming."

"He knew she was a little girl?"

"He knew she was four years old," she says.

"Maybe this was Roosevelt's plan in the first place."

Nicolas loads in the backpacks.

On the bank above the river, Rosie calls for help decamping and Georgie heads up the hill to pack up the tent where Rosie and Venus slept, slipping Rosie's backpack over her shoulder. She helps Venus push the second canoe into the water — the river quiet this morning as the sun rises, water

214

lazily slapping the bank.

It is still early, not yet six-thirty.

Long, long summer days in Northern Wisconsin.

She walks upriver where Nicolas is packing his canoe.

"I don't think I told him Oona's name," she says almost to herself. "Or maybe I did. What difference does it make if he knows her name?"

What time had it been last night or early this morning when she and Thomas heard the bear who was not a bear thumping next to Oona's tent?

It could not have been an animal that took her away. It had to be a human. A thumping human.

Oona would have screamed out and they would have heard her unless something were stuffed in her mouth. Or a hand across her lips.

"Roosevelt knew about everyone who was going to be on this trip with us," Georgie says to Nicolas, keeping her voice low, slow, so it won't quiver. "I told him. I told him about you."

"Great, Georgie. One good fucking idea after the next."

Nicolas climbs into the stern, slaps his paddle on the surface of the water.

"Get into the boat, Venus, and no woo-woo advice. You're paddling bow."

Venus has been silent, but she touches Georgie's arm as she walks past her.

"Later," she says.

"You're going to walk that dirt path behind the wheelbarrow and hope to find town?" Rosie asks.

"I am."

"You're sure there is a town?"

"I'm not sure, but there's a small round brown circle on the map — that has to be town."

"Are you hopeful, Mama?" she asks under her breath.

"I am hopeful."

"Missing is the worst, isn't it?" Rosie says in that way she sometimes has of giving voice to the truth. "Worse than dead."

She doesn't cry. Not when she was a child, not even when Richard died and never in the months that he was ill, but she is weeping now and that is more unbearable to Georgie than her own fear.

As if Rosie knows something that she does not.

Jesse lowers himself into the stern of the second canoe, his paddle in the water. Bent over, he puts his head on his knees.

"How will we be in touch?" Rosie calls.

"We can't," Georgie says. "We have to count on each other's good sense."

"Roosevelt will save our lives," Nicolas calls. "He'll be sitting at a picnic table with Oona beside him, and when he sees us pull up, he'll yell *Hi, guys,* like a regular run-of-the-mill pedophile."

He pushes the boat away from the bank with his paddle.

"Two hours, Georgie?" he asks.

"That is what we were told," Georgie says.

She watches the canoes turn into the current.

"Nobody even asked if I would come along with them," Thomas says as the canoes head upriver, the water barely slapping the bank.

"We're the only ones who wanted to come on this trip, Thomas. You and me. Just you and me."

■ ■ ■ ■

CAMP
MINNIE HAHA

■ ■ ■ ■

June 18, 2008

ROOSEVELT

It is just after eight in the morning when Georgie's family arrives at Camp Minnie HaHa and turns the canoes into the still-water cove. A dock with a diving board extends over the river, the buildings of the camp on a hill above the shore.

Roosevelt McCrary stands at the end of the dock, his arms folded across his chest, a black and white Australian shepherd lying at his feet.

"There he is," Venus says to no one in particular.

They pull the two canoes across the shallow water and tie up at the bank.

"I was doing okay," Nicolas says, leaning into Rosie. "Now I can hardly breathe."

Rosie wraps her arm around his back.

"It was kind of a relief paddling — but now the air is gone so *you* tell Roosevelt about Oona," Nicolas says. "I can't."

"I will tell him."

"Tell him he's ruining my life and I'm likely to take a swing at him."

"Don't!" Rosie tightens her arm around his back, sensing that Nicolas might — it was altogether possible — actually hit Roosevelt.

"When we find Oona," he says. "I'm on the next plane home."

Fog is lifting off the horizon to a brightening day, the ground still damp with dew, the air sharp and chilly.

Roosevelt is tall and straight-backed, with thick white hair and hazel eyes more green than brown. Youthful in jeans, muddy at the knees, a red flannel shirt under a blue sweater, heavy hiking boots.

Rosie pulls herself onto the dock, reaching out her hand to him.

"We're Georgie's children," she says.

"I'm glad to see you!"

His deep rich voice surprises her.

"Is this everyone?"

"Except Georgie who isn't here with us," Rosie says. "She's at the campground looking for Oona."

"Her granddaughter?"

"Yes, her granddaughter. She disappeared from her tent in the middle of the night."

"Disappeared?"

"She was in a tent alone and sleeping and

Georgie was close by talking with my son, but at dawn when Thomas woke up, Oona was gone."

"Around midnight, they heard a loud noise in the brush — and thought maybe *a bear,*" Venus says stepping on the dock beside her sister. "But a bear wouldn't go in a tent to steal a child."

"We have bears," Roosevelt says. "But no . . ." His voice trails off.

"The cell phones don't work, so there was no way to get in touch with anyone. We had to come here to find you," Venus says.

Nicolas has not moved from the bank, where he stands with Jesse — slouched, his back to them.

"Georgie is hoping you can help us," Venus says.

"You haven't notified the police?" Roosevelt asks.

"We can't because of the cell phones. No one around to help," Nicolas says, turning toward the dock. "As far as I can tell, no one even lives in Wisconsin except *you.*"

Roosevelt steps off to the bank.

"I'll call the police on the land line now," he says, a hand lightly on Nicolas' shoulder.

"Georgie promised the phones *would* work or I certainly would not be in the state of Wisconsin at all," Nicolas says, stepping

223

just clear of Roosevelt's hand on his shoulder. "Like everything about my mother's plan for this trip, she was wrong."

"I'll call the river police from the landline in the lodge and also the police in the town of Riverton, which is the closest precinct to Missing Lake."

"Are they competent?" Nicolas asks.

"They're as good as we have," Roosevelt says. "I also *know* people in the town of Missing Lake. One man in particular, the pharmacist, and I'll call him from the lodge."

He raises his arm indicating for them to follow him up the hill, the dog ambling at his side.

"Mercy," he says. "I call all my dogs Mercy."

He has a slight limp, holding one hip with his large hand as if to keep it in place as he walks up the hill, craggy ground with rocks, balancing with a cane.

The lodge is long, a two-story log structure on a rise above the river, the cabins beyond. The main room is vaulted, with a line of windows overlooking the water and a walk-in fireplace banked but unlit — rough-hewn wooden tables and benches, the walls unfinished pine with group photographs of past campers dating back to the summer of 1909.

They pull out the benches and sit at the table nearest to the fireplace, Nicolas leaning against the stone mantel.

The table is set — wildflowers in a jar — cloth napkins.

"I've got breakfast ready, but first I'm calling the police."

"Call fast," Nicolas says. "Oona is not the kind of four-year-old who just gets lost. Anything could have happened."

"They will find her," Roosevelt says. "Missing Lake is not a town for trouble. Not criminal trouble"

"So what kind of town is it?" Venus asks.

"It's an isolated place with ordinary people — a little depressed. They drink too much, but only at night and especially in the winter when it's always dark."

"Just call the police and the guy you know in Missing Lake," Nicolas says. "I'm not an optimist. That's my mother's occupation."

Roosevelt goes up the steps by the fireplace and closes the door at the landing.

"He's kind of sweet," Venus says.

"After three minutes?" Nicolas says. "I don't have a lot of confidence in your character assessments."

"I agree with Venus," Rosie says. "He

seems . . . I don't know. Gentle, I guess."

"At least he's not a pedophile." Jesse rests his head in his arms, his baseball cap pulled down over his eyes. "That's what Rosie means."

"Where did you pick up the word *pedophile*, Jesse?"

"That was your description of Roosevelt this morning, Dad."

"Well don't use it. Don't use *fuck* either."

"I never do."

They sit around the table waiting, trying to think of something, anything, to say into the stillness of the room.

Anything to alleviate the hollow echoes in the vast damp loneliness of the lodge.

Nicolas paces the fireplace from one side to the other, his hands fisted — hitting the jagged stone with his right hand until it's bloody, hitting the same place each time so the stone is bloody. He stops and licks the blood from his hand.

"Dad!" Jesse says. "Don't drink your own blood."

"He needs to, Jesse," Venus says. "He needs to go back and forth and back and forth and hit the stone so it cuts his hand. A pattern. I get it."

"What is taking that guy so long," Jesse asks.

"Roosevelt," Rosie says. "Not *that guy.*"

"I know," Jesse says. "Roosevelt."

"I hear him coming now," Venus says. "His heavy boots."

Roosevelt comes through the door and down the steps, Mercy beside him.

Under his arm, he has a roll of paper — long — the size of a large map.

"Did you find out anything?" Rosie asks.

"No concrete news, but I got the police. This is the first they heard she was missing, but they told me they'll be back in touch as soon as they know anything."

He sets the roll of paper on the table and goes into the kitchen, soon bringing out a tray of hot blueberry muffins and waffles.

"You don't know anything else?" Venus asks.

"That's it. I have suspicions but no evidence. And the police aren't interested in suspicions right now. My guess is the river police are already patrolling and likely at the campsite."

"We're interested in suspicions, so what do you suspect?" Rosie asks.

"Just ordinary suspicions a person has if you've lived in a place for a long time, especially isolated like this," he says unrolling the map, anchoring it with two glass pitchers.

"Help yourself to breakfast."

He leans over the table, the map under his hand — Jesse and Rosie beside him.

"Just so you can see the topography of the campsite at Missing Lake."

"Nicolas?" Rosie calls.

Nicolas has moved away from the fireplace across the room to the windows overlooking the Bone River, standing with his back to them, very still, his forehead against the window pane.

"Here is where you were last night," Roosevelt is saying, pointing to the campsite. "On this section of the river you can only access civilization on the east bank by walking this path — he points to the path behind the campsite. "The path is overgrown and rocky, but it goes to the town of Missing Lake about three miles east of the campsite. The forest that surrounds the path is too dense to navigate. There're fallen trees and branches and thick underbrush. It's wilderness really on both sides of the river."

He puts his hands in the pockets of his jeans. "That's why it's difficult in this part of Wisconsin to be in touch when there's an emergency."

"I guess Georgie didn't ask that question when she made reservations with the outfitters," Rosie says.

"What I can tell you about the campsite at Missing Lake is that it would be almost impossible for a person to penetrate the woods," Roosevelt says. "They'd need to come from the town of Missing Lake on foot and with intention."

"What are you saying?" Rosie asks.

"I'm saying that very likely, unless a little girl decided to walk to Missing Lake alone at night, the person who took her from the tent is from the town of Missing Lake three miles out from the campsite."

"Kidnapped, not took," Venus says.

"Do you know anyone who lives in Missing Lake?" Jesse asks.

"I do," Roosevelt says rolling the map, sticking it under his arm. "I know everyone there."

Nicolas has moved away from the window, pacing the length of the lodge in flip-flops so the rubber slaps against the floor with every step he takes.

"Breakfast?" Roosevelt asks him as Venus and Rosie slip into the benches around the table.

"I don't want breakfast," Nicolas says.

"Nothing?" Roosevelt asks. "Not coffee?"

"Nothing."

"This is going to drive me crazy," Venus says. "We have to eat, Nicolas."

"I don't blame him. He's too upset to eat," Roosevelt says, taking a seat at the table next to Rosie. "What about Jesse?" he asks of Jesse, who lies on the couch in front of the fireplace, a baseball cap covering his face.

Rosie shakes her head.

"I doubt he'll eat."

"You used the word *suspicion*," Venus says. "What do you mean by that?"

"Not really a suspicion," Roosevelt says. "Missing Lake is an odd town, out of touch with the world."

"Is there anyone in particular you think could be suspicious?" Rosie asks.

"Possibly," he hesitates, clearing his throat. "There is a woman in town who got pregnant by the pharmacist some years ago and the child was stillborn. She went a little crazy after the child was dead."

"Are you suggesting that she would take a child out of a tent in the middle of the night?" Rosie asks.

"I suppose that is what I'm saying. She's not . . ." He pauses, considering. "She's not exactly normal."

The *slap-slap-slap* of flip-flops ceases and Nicolas, standing just beyond the table, is listening.

"She pretends her baby is alive and growing up," he says, pouring more coffee. "Her house in the Shallows behind town is filled with children's books and toys and clothes on hangers."

"Poor girl," Venus says.

"But there isn't anything *bad* about her. Just missing parts in her brain."

"She sounds obsessive," Venus says. "I know about obsessive because I am one. Reformed."

"Are you saying this woman you know about with a child fetish is mentally ill?" Nicolas asks.

"She *is*. Mentally ill but harmless."

"How can you say harmless?" Nicolas asks. "Who knows about harmless in another person?"

"I know," Roosevelt says. "She wouldn't hurt a child."

"Fuck!" Nicolas slams his already-bloody fist into the stone fireplace again and again. "A child safe with a mentally ill woman? Bad thinking," he says to Roosevelt. "This place is insane."

"Don't break your hand, Dad." Jesse covers his ears.

"I want to break my hand," Nicolas says.

Roosevelt heads into the kitchen, Mercy at his heels.

"I trust him, Nicolas," Rosie says. "I have

231

an instinct."

"So do I," Venus says.

Nicolas slips to the floor, his back to the fireplace, his head resting on his knees, his injured hand weeping blood.

"I hope he doesn't bang his head against the fireplace," Venus whispers across the table.

His long, low growl fills the room.

"I can't stand to watch him." Venus covers her eyes.

At the top of the steps, Roosevelt stops, shaking his head.

"This is an awful introduction to all of you," he says. "I am so sorry."

He sits on the bench beside Rosie and lays his hand on top of hers.

"Tell us about Missing Lake," Venus says, tears running down her cheeks. "Just talk so there will be another sound in the room besides Nicolas."

Roosevelt rests his elbows on the table.

"Is it just a regular small midwestern town near a river?" she asks.

"It's too remote to be an altogether ordinary place," he says. "Young people used to go along that path behind the campsite — it's the only way to get to the river from the town and when they got to the river, they did bad things."

"Like what?"

"Sex, alcohol, probably drugs. A boy died once swimming with too much to drink."

"Could there have been teenage boys last night?" Rosie asks.

"That's not possible — there are no teenage boys," Roosevelt says. "A few years ago, the women left. They packed their belongings, took their children, left their husbands or boyfriends or took them along, but most of the men were not willing to go."

"Why?" Venus asks.

"The women were bored, the kids were bored, the men spent the evenings at the pool hall or the bar. It's that kind of place."

"No children? No women at all?" Rosie asks

"A few women like the woman I mentioned, but no children at all," he says. "The school closed down. Now it's just this place where I go to get supplies and hardware and leave when I'm done shopping."

He gets up to pour more coffee.

"And no black people live there," he says. "That's another thing."

"Why does the woman you mentioned stay there if most of the women have left?" Rosie asks.

"She has her reasons."

"So you know her?" Venus asks.

"I do."

Roosevelt speaks slowly and with care.

"I know her well enough not to worry that she will harm anyone but herself," he says.

Nicolas, holding his injured hand, collapses on the bench at the far end of the table.

"Do *you* know about our family?" Rosie asks.

"Only William," Roosevelt says.

"Georgie knows nothing about her father," Rosie says. "Did she tell you that? Nothing. He left a letter for her just before he died. That's all. One letter from prison."

"I was fifteen when William died in prison in 1945," Roosevelt says. "The owners of the camp — one was William's uncle Irving — invited me back then. But I didn't come, and later I did."

"It seems like a strange place for you to land," Rosie says.

"Strange, yes — for a man like me from Washington, D.C," he says. "My mother and William were close. He lived for a while at his uncle's house, where she was a cook, and before she died, she told me stories about him."

"What do you remember about him?" Venus asks.

Roosevelt hesitates, resting his chin in his

hand, looking off into the middle distance before he speaks.

"A lot," he says. "When a person you love dies, you remember what you need to remember to keep him in your life."

"You *loved* him?" Rosie asks.

"I did."

Roosevelt sets a plate of waffles on the floor for Mercy.

"She's fifteen. I give her whatever she wants," he says.

He kisses the top of her head.

"You were at the campsite when Georgie's mother died?" Nicolas asks, subdued, holding his injured hand.

"Murdered," Roosevelt says, as if the fact of it still surprises him. "I wrote Georgianna a letter for her birthday."

"She read the letter at the birthday dinner she gave for herself," Nicolas says, shaking his head. "You would have thought . . ."

"We've seen the story in the *Chicago Tribune,*" Venus says.

"Your mother's name is on the list of people who were at the campsite," Rosie says, "but I guess you were too young to be mentioned by name."

"I was mentioned. Negro boy child, age 11," he says. "My mother had that paper and I read it too."

He pours more coffee from a blue and white enamel coffee pot, spilling just a little with each cup.

"How well did you know him?"

"I knew him well," he says. "I was a baby and without a father when William came from Lithuania to live at his uncle's house, where my mother and grandmother worked."

"Georgie has no idea you knew him well unless you told her," Rosie says.

"I didn't tell her," he says. "I have waited until we are face-to-face."

Roosevelt wipes down the table, carries the dishes to the kitchen, stacks the glasses in the sink. Rosie leans against the kitchen door, Venus at the sink washing.

He reaches in his pocket, takes out a cheese stick, dips it in the pitcher of maple syrup and drops it in Mercy's mouth.

"She eats well," he says.

"Do you ever think about what happened when our grandmother was killed?" Rosie asks.

"I think about it all the time. Even now after so many years, I still think about it."

"Did Georgie tell you that she believes her father was innocent?" Rosie asks.

"She thinks he was protecting someone else and that's why he confessed to a murder he didn't commit," Venus says.

"Well . . ." But the telephone is ringing and Roosevelt heads to the office. "I'm guessing it's the police," he says. "I'll be right back."

"We'll finish the dishes."

Venus turns on the hot water and sprays the plates.

"There are beds for you up the stairs from the kitchen," Roosevelt says, closing the office door. "Make yourself at home."

"What are you thinking?" Venus asks when the phone stops ringing.

"What else to think about but Oona," Rosie says.

"I have bad feelings." Venus leans against the sink.

"Don't tell Nicolas," Rosie says.

They finish washing the dishes, drying them, putting them on the open shelves, and come back to the table.

When Roosevelt comes down the steps from the office, he is carrying a large framed photograph.

"News?" Venus asks.

"The river police from Riverton went in motorboats to search the banks of the river, and they're there now," Roosevelt says. "The police report that the campsite is empty. There's no canoe. No evidence of camping."

"That means Georgie must have left the campsite, right?" Nicolas lifts his head.

"Someone had to take the canoe," he says.

"If that's the case, I bet she's found Oona," Rosie says. "Otherwise she wouldn't leave."

"Or not," Venus says. "The police might have told her that they have the kidnapping covered and Georgie should get in the canoe and come here."

"I think you're wrong," Rosie says.

Roosevelt puts the photograph down on the counter.

"Your grandfather," he says.

They have only seen one photograph of William, and that sits on the round table in Georgie's bedroom, likely taken at camp. He is leaning against the large trunk of a deciduous tree, shadows of leaves across his shirt.

In the present photograph on the counter, William is on the porch of the lodge, his arms folded across his chest, a stripe of light across his torso. He's wearing shorts, a collared shirt with the sleeves rolled up, unsmiling, his expression serious, his large, dark eyes intense.

On the copper plate affixed to the bottom

of the frame and written in small block letters — WILLIAM GROVE, DIRECTOR CAMP MINNIE HAHA, SUMMER 1939.

"I discovered this photograph among a lot of photographs of your grandfather, but this one looks just like William as I remember him, so I had it framed for my office and had the metal plate made to honor him." Roosevelt says. "I don't know if it was taken in 1939, but that was the year I was nine and William sent me a birthday card with two fifty-dollar bills. I'd never seen a fifty-dollar bill."

He takes the photograph into the main room and rests it against the wall on the mantel.

"I'll leave it here for Georgianna when she comes."

"Which could be soon," Rosie says.

"Then we should go down to the river and wait for her to arrive." Roosevelt checks his watch. "Surely if the canoe is gone from the campsite, she should be headed here."

Nicolas sits up on the couch, his phone in his good hand. Jesse beside him.

"Any luck with reception?" Roosevelt asks.

"Nothing."

"You should go to the end of the diving board and try it."

"What makes you think that?"

"Parents when they come to bring their kids to camp have told me they occasionally get reception late morning at the end of the diving board." He shrugs. "Who knows? I don't have a cell phone."

It's cool near the river, and the sun, halfway to noon, deconstructs the landscape with light. Warm on their faces. Nicolas has walked back to the dock and is sitting on the end of the diving board swinging his legs.

"Have a chair," Roosevelt says, indicating the Adirondacks lined up on the bank of the river.

Venus lies on the grass, her arm over her eyes to keep out the sun.

"Have you called Mom?" Jesse calls to his father.

He is sitting beside Venus.

"Dad?"

"No reason to upset her until I have something to say," Nicolas says.

"But you have something to say," Jesse says.

"Yes, I do. But it's something upsetting."

"Do you have a cigarette?" Jesse asks Venus.

"I'm a reformed addict. I don't have anything but squished M&M's."

"May I have those?"

She hands him the flattened package of regular M&M's.

"I'm sorry, Jesse," she says gently.

"I didn't even like Oona very much until she disappeared," he says.

Rosie kicks off her flip-flops and stretches out next to Jesse, leaning up against him.

"They'll be okay," she says.

"Who?" Jesse asks. "Thomas?"

"And Georgie and Oona."

"Georgie knows what she is doing," Jesse says.

"Georgie?" Nicolas says. "What makes you think that Georgie knows what she's doing?"

"She's just the kind of person who knows things," Jesse says.

"Sometimes," Venus says, "and sometimes she doesn't."

She wraps her arms around her knees.

"This promises to be the longest day in my life," Nicolas says.

"Well, I trust Georgie," Jesse is saying.

"We trust Georgie too," Rosie says. "It's just that we didn't exactly want to come on this trip and it turns out that we were right."

"But we're here," Venus says. "And you've got to admit that when we find Oona, it'll be kind of cool that we're here at the place

Georgie has always thought of as Home with this old guy who seems perfectly fine, perfectly ordinary, not at all some kind of Svengali, right? And handsome!"

"Drop it, Venus," Nicolas says.

There's a long silence, Venus struggling to fill it, but she cannot think of what to say.

"I do not have a cigarette, Venus," Nicolas says.

"I didn't ask for one."

That is where they are for the time being, Rosie tells Venus. *Their life as a family has turned a corner to something else.*

If Oona is gone, actually gone, *they will never be that family again.*

"I don't understand Georgie sometimes," Venus says. "I mean I'm a true believer in the stars and she's a scientist. But to reenact a murder the way she set this up with all of us — matching the day and the place and the circumstances. It's disturbing!"

"Do you think we're going to be okay?" Jesse asks. "All of us?"

"Okay? Who knows?"

"Hush, Venus," Rosie says. "We *will* be okay, Jesse."

Nicolas is pacing up and down the diving board.

"Dad's on the phone!" Jesse calls out. "He's got a connection. Did you hear the phone ring?"

"I didn't," Venus says.

"Shut the fuck up," Nicolas shouts suddenly.

"I beg your pardon?" Venus says.

"Mom." Jesse says quietly.

"Mom?" Venus asks.

"He's talking to Olivia."

Roosevelt has come around the lodge and is heading down the hill. He stops at the bank, waits, his hands in his pockets, looking out over the river, checking his watch.

"Thunder," he says to no one in particular, but Venus overhears him.

"Thunder?" she asks. "I don't hear it."

"In the distance. South," he says. "Maybe it will roll in or maybe not."

Nicolas is still on the phone, sitting at the end of the diving board.

I know, I know, I know, Olivia, he is saying when Roosevelt comes up behind them.

"Just a second," he says to Roosevelt. "Goodbye, Olivia. I will call as soon as I have news. We will find her."

We will find her.

He is almost screaming.

He walks back to the bank, where his family is now stretched out on the grass.

"News?" he asks.

"Only this," Roosevelt says. "The pharma-

243

cist was on the camp phone again. He called about the murder."

"What murder?" Venus asks. "How many murders can there be around here?"

"The only murder. The one in 1941. They are interested that I was at the campsite when Georgianna's mother was murdered."

"That was years ago," Rosie says.

"People don't have much to think about in Missing Lake," Roosevelt says.

"I wonder if the people in town knew that we were coming?" Venus asks. "If word got around that the Grove family would be here for the first time *ever* since it happened."

"They knew," Roosevelt says, crouching down, his arm flung around Mercy.

"How did they know?" Rosie asks. "From Georgie?"

"Not from Georgie. Mr. Blake didn't know who Georgie was when she called to reserve the trip."

He nestles his face in Mercy's fur and stands, slowly, the rising of an aging man with a large frame.

A long quiet as he looks out over the river, the sun in a westward descent, a dark cloud hovering in the distance, a light chop on the water.

"People knew you were coming because I told them."

■ ■ ■ ■

MISSING LAKE

■ ■ ■ ■

June 18, 2008

GEORGIANNA

Georgie picks up her backpack and slips her arm through the straps.

Just after seven now and the sun is lifting over the pines, the pines thick with scent and dampness taking up space in her head — she can actually feel it, demons crowding the recreation room of her brain where she counts on her imagination to be at work.

"What is a pedophile, Georgie?"

"Nicolas will say *anything* when he's upset."

"It means something."

"It means *nothing* to us," Georgie says.

They head up the hill, past Oona's tent, past the red wheelbarrow and into the pine forest.

"I want to talk about Oona."

"We're not going to talk about Oona," she says. "We're not going to talk."

"All I want to ask you is why was it so important for Oona to come on this trip which she won't even remember because she's only four."

"There's nothing to say about Oona."

The path to Missing Lake is slippery and wet, roots protruding and rocks, the rotting smell of fungi in the air.

Georgie goes to the edge of the forest standing beside Thomas.

"Here is where I'm looking," he says.

He ducks under the branches of a high pine.

"No one could possibly get through here. It's too dense."

He tries to push into the underbrush, but the low branches of pine slap his face, the undergrowth thick and tough-skinned. He drops to his hands and knees inching over the roots, the fallen branches.

"Oona's little enough to get through," he calls. "She could be in the deep wood."

"Why would she do that, Thomas. Especially in darkness?"

"I'll go just a little further."

A large spindly branched fir scrapes across his skin drawing blood, and he lies flat, wriggles into the clearing.

"You're bleeding."

"I know I'm bleeding," he says. "I don't mind blood, but can I ask you just this one thing?"

Georgie puts her hands over her ears, so that any sound, even that of the river, is a low din rolling in the distance and all she can hear alone with herself is the sound of her own body vibrating as if it is about to explode.

She cannot have a panic attack. Not now. Not with so much immediately at stake.

"Thomas?"

He is walking ahead of her now, wiping the blood off his face with the sleeve of his sweatshirt.

"You asked why I wanted especially to have Oona here?" She catches up to him. "The answer is not an answer you'll understand since even I don't understand it."

"Tell me anyway."

"I wanted everyone on this trip, but in particular I wanted Oona. I wanted to have a sense of four years old. I have wondered what is it like to *be* four and how did I make it through what happened," she says. "Or did I."

"I don't understand," he says. "I'm only thirteen."

The path from the campsite packed down from rains is easy walking except for the rocks and exposed roots. Mainly pine needles, black soil, a layer of rotting leaves. No evident footsteps or bear paws or clear signs of passage along the route.

Except, suddenly, just beyond the clearing, a footprint.

A muddy heel.

Certainly it is a heel, perhaps from a boot. Maybe a shoe but more likely a heavy boot by the depth of it on the wet ground.

She squats to get a closer look.

"A footprint?" Thomas asks.

He leans down beside her.

"It's got to be a boot."

"Are there more footprints ahead?" she asks, crouching beside him.

Thomas walks ahead, his eyes peeled on the ground, but it's dark on the path, the pine trees high and thick, cutting out the light from the rising sun.

"Walk along the edge so you don't step on any evidence in case there are more footsteps."

"I don't see any more," he calls.

"Odd," Georgie says. "One footprint." What could have happened to the other foot?"

"At least we know it's a new footprint, so someone has been on this path recently."

She turns back to the boot print, kneeling beside it.

A man's boot heel. Only one. She is thinking what might have happened. *Was he carrying Oona? Holding her arms or perhaps her arms were tied so she could not yank out the cloth — maybe a handkerchief — stuffed in her mouth so she couldn't scream.*

"You're sure it's the footprint of a man?" Thomas asks.

"I am *sure* of nothing. But the footprint is fresh and I am guessing it belongs to the person who took Oona."

"What if she went to the river on a whim?" Thomas asks. "Or else it was a bear."

"Not a bear, Thomas. And I don't think Oona walked out of the tent and went to the river. She was barefoot. I checked the path from the tent when we were putting in the boats just now. No little feet."

"She had on socks."

"There still would have been evidence of little feet. The ground is muddy, especially at the top of the embankment where her tent was pitched."

Oona is not a child who would walk down to the river in the dark.

Or fall in the water.

But what can Georgie really *know*. What does anyone know about another person. Even about a child.

She can only trust what is necessary to believe for finding Oona.

Which is that Oona is somewhere close by and on land and has not fallen into the river and drowned.

That is the reasonable way to think about finding Oona.

"So what now?" Thomas asks.

"We keep walking," Georgie says.

"What if there is nothing?"

"There will be something."

So they walk.

Slowly, with their eyes on the ground as the sun rises higher in the sky and the light through the trees brightens the path on which they are traveling.

The route bends to the right, narrows, closes in on them so they must go single-file through an opening in the trees, across logs over a slow stream into a clearing.

In the middle of the clearing, a branch, Georgie's height, stuck in the ground at an angle and wrapped around the top with a green ribbon, an actual ribbon.

"*Grosgrain,*" Georgie says aloud. "Who in the woods has grosgrain ribbon in his pocket?"

"What do you think?" Thomas asks.

"I don't know what to think," Georgie says getting down on her knees to examine the branch and the ground around it. "Somebody put it here, but I don't know where here is.

"Maybe we're close to the town."

"Maybe," Georgie says

She puts her hands in her pockets and stretches her back.

She feels too fragile.

Through the years, she has developed ways to slow her mind, to keep fear in the dark by dwelling on the small topographical details of a landscape, especially in Africa. The clump of poison ivy, the way pine roots resurface at surprising distances, splashes of white daisylike flowers, lacing through the ground cover in the wood.

She has been afraid, but never with the sense she has now that she could crumble as if her skeleton has gone soft and porous.

When Charley was killed, she was ready for the news. She had gone through his dying night after night in the months before he died.

But this is different;

Keep moving, she thinks. Just the process of walking — one foot in front of the next, swinging her arms as if to propel her body forward. Even that promises an arrival someplace and someplace is better than no place at all.

No place at all would be losing Oona.

"Does it seem crazy to you walking

through the woods like this as if we're going to find her someplace along the way?"

Thomas falls in step.

"It's the only thing we can do now," Georgie says.

"What if there isn't a town?"

"If not a town, there has to be a place," she says.

For so many summers, Georgie has lived in remote places, mainly Botswana with the Baos tribe — places where there isn't a path to anywhere, no real roads, just a settlement sprouting in the middle of the jungle or the rain forest or by a river.

Occasionally, not often, she has been panicked — as if dropped in a place where no one can see her. Where she has no sense of being. No existence.

But this is home. America. Wisconsin. Civilization crowding in just beyond her view. Surely a place will materialize — a village, a town, a filling station where she will find information.

"Oona must be terrified," Thomas says.

"She must be."

I was only four.

Too young to understand that the present may be temporary but what happens in the present remains.

A story is unrolling in her mind.

Oona sleeping with Freddy, cozy in the sleeping bag waiting for Thomas to crawl in beside her, his head on the same pillow.

And then something. A sound. A displacement of air. A body.

Georgie imagines there is a man who has Oona in mind. He is walking the same path on which she and Thomas are now walking, watching from a distance by the raw light of the moon. His eye is on the tent with Oona sleeping alone. He has been watching and knows she is there and sleeping alone.

The man crouches, enters in the darkness through the flap so quietly Georgie and Thomas are unaware until that one moment when they hear the bear who was not a bear.

In the distance, the sound of a truck. A screech of brakes. A low sharp horn, three blasts and silence.

Ahead the path ends.

Thomas is walking a few feet in front of Georgie when he suddenly stops and turns.

"Someone," he says.

"Someone?"

"There."

Someone has stepped out of the shadowed darkness onto the path scattered now with sunlight.

A woman by the size of her, though maybe a man.

She is standing on the path in front of them blocking their way. Her hands at her side, her feet apart, a wool cap on the back of her head.

Georgie catches up.

"I can't see," she says, her eyes adjusting to the light just beyond where what looks to be a town has appeared.

"Don't worry." It *is* a woman with a gravelly cigarette voice. "You don't need to see."

She steps toward Georgie.

"I know who you are. I've known about you all my life," the woman says. "Do not get near me. I have a gun."

She is not holding the gun but her hand is at her hip, resting on the pocket of her shorts.

Georgie folds her arms tight across her chest as if to contain her heart.

Something familiar about this woman. Her black hair hanging like so many ribbons over her shoulders, her eyes sunken in a hard face burned by the sun. Or drink or cigarettes or life. A wasted face older than fifty perhaps. Or not.

She could be handsome. She is tall with strong, bold features. Slender.

The woman glances into the forest.

"So you," she says. "Come out. And don't talk."

Nothing comes from the forest but a rustle of pine needles.

"Now," the woman says. "Come out *now.*"

The branches part, a small arm through the brush. A child.

Thomas grips Georgie's shoulder, but she has already seen the child.

Oona in her yellow bear pajamas, her black hair tangled, her eyes wide.

Thomas makes a move, but the woman reaches into her pocket.

"Don't even try," she says. "This is my child now. That's why I have a gun."

"We won't give you trouble," Georgie says quietly.

"Don't talk to the child. One word and it's a big problem for you."

Oona is silent looking directly at Georgie, but her eyes are flat as though she cannot see.

The woman reaches down and takes Oona's hand.

"Turn around towards the campsite now. You two, turn around. I'm behind you and if you run . . ." A deep laugh. "Nevermind. You won't."

They walk along the path — slowly, since

Georgie is in the lead sensing something could happen if Oona cannot keep up.

She can hear the crush of pine needles behind them, the occasional soft whimper, the muffled *shhh,* but she and Thomas look ahead.

"Shut up," the woman says. "Shut up your whining."

Thomas' arm brushes Georgie's and he leans against her shoulder.

They could die here, Georgie is thinking. If the woman does have a gun and they upset her. If she is crazy. She could be out of her mind, the way her eyes are lit with fury. Or possibly fear. Or — *chaos* is the word that comes to mind.

No one is around. No one likely to be wandering on the dense pine path early in the morning. When they arrive at the campsite, if that is the plan the woman has in mind, Georgie's children will have already left for Minnie HaHa and nothing in the geography of Missing Lake seems to promise rescue.

Georgie has no real memory of what happened on the morning after her mother was murdered.

She would have been somewhere at the campsite — only so much land to occupy in the half-moon of Missing Lake.

She has an image of herself inside a tent with a woman, perhaps the nurse — she knows from the newspaper that the camp nurse was at Missing Lake. The nurse is reading a book to her while Georgie examines her arms that have broken out with a red itchy rash. The woman says *No scratching* and the words *No scratching* always accompany the memory.

Even now Georgie has an occasional physical sensation on her skin as if a colony of small insects is running up and down her arms. Occasionally a rash will surface, but it comes and goes. She feels it now sizzling along the surface of her skin and pulls up the sleeve of her turtleneck to check if her arm is mottled red.

But it is not.

"What are you doing?" the woman asks.

"I'm checking a rash I sometimes get."

"Well don't check it again."

The only emotion that Georgie has ever imagined that morning of her mother's murder is terror. But terror is simply a word. Not something she can call up from memory.

There must have been a buzz of activity — of police and boats with emergency medical personnel and counselors gathered in small, hushed groups, filling the air with muted sounds of terror.

For all her travels in Africa, Georgie has never experienced that.

Close calls — almost every summer there was something. But never terror.

Now walking on the path toward the Bone River, Georgie is dissembling like the legos that Thomas used to construct as a little boy and then with a slash of his arm destroy.

She takes a deep breath, lets the air out slowly.

"Don't hold hands," the woman behind them calls out. "It's making me nervous. Nervous is not good."

The sun is moving overhead, the morning warming, and Georgie pulls off her turtleneck, a tee shirt underneath and underneath that a camisole, no bra. She tucks the tee shirt into her jeans and ties the turtleneck around her waist.

"I was too hot," she says in explanation, but the woman does not respond.

Only halfway back to the river now and then what? Will they stop someplace along the way? Will the woman wait until they reach the campsite and then *something* will happen?

To Georgie and Thomas. To Oona?

Unimaginable what the woman has in mind.

"Fill up your mind," Georgie whispers to Thomas.

"Shut up," the woman says. "I told you not to talk. I meant don't talk at all."

The air is suddenly cold. Shortly after nine and clouds must be floating across the sun, the light filtered in the forest, a chill up Georgie's spine and she finds herself off balance, the ground uneven enough to trip her and tripping could lead to a fall and falling as she read just recently in the *New York Times* — it actually stopped her and she read it twice — is the second-leading cause of death in people over sixty.

She cannot die now at this moment.

Gone and then what? Who will be there to help her family if she has the carelessness to die in these woods?

"Better not do something to make me nervous," the woman calls out. "Nervous I'm dangerous. You'll see."

Georgie keeps her eyes peeled to the ground. High tree roots breaking through the earth. Unexpected dips in the land. A hidden animal hole.

"Listen, you folks, just sit in the corner of your own minds and have a conversation with yourself and leave me be," the woman says. "Got it?"

Thomas nods.

"You got it too — Professor Georgianna Grove — daughter of a murderer?"

How did she know? How could she, this woman with a gun, possibly know about Georgianna Grove.

Nicolas was right of course. Nicolas is always right.

Why did Georgie need to come to Missing Lake, Wisconsin, to stand on the same earth where her mother had been strangled? She could have gone by van to Camp Minnie HaHa to meet Roosevelt McCrary there and skip Missing Lake altogether.

It is beginning to rain, mist settling on her body and her face — rain without weight or even drops, as if the dampness were coming from inside of her.

Georgie looks over at Thomas. His profile, his articulated nose and heavy brow, his forehead wrinkled in a frown, his bottom lip protruding as if he were about to cry.

But he will not cry.

She cannot seem to put a stop to memories of death, as if a pattern were preordained in the texture of her psyche, and what had begun in Georgie's life when her mother was murdered set up the markers for endings, one after the other, up to this moment on the path to Missing Lake.

It is cooler than it was and cloudy. Not chilly, but Georgie is cold. She wraps her arms around herself, her shoulders lifted, her chin down.

At the top of the incline ahead, against a backdrop of the black trunks of pine trees and glistening in the sun — the red wheelbarrow.

"You see that?" the woman asks.

"Yes," Georgie says.

"It's mine," she says. "I brought it here because I thought the place needed a little color." She hesitates. "Don't bother to add your two bits."

Georgie walks past the wheelbarrow to the one remaining tent where Oona had been sleeping and stops, Thomas beside her whispering something she cannot hear.

"Go into the tent now. Both of you," the woman says. "Go in and sit down and shut up and I'll be out here with my child."

It occurs to Georgie that the woman has a plan.

But maybe not.

Maybe the tent is simply a way station while she decides what next.

Maybe there is no plan at all.

Just a gun and Oona.

When Georgie and Thomas came down the path, the woman must not have expected them. Wherever she was planning to take Oona or for whatever reason, she must have believed she'd been successful in capturing the little girl and would have time to execute her plan.

"Did you hear me? Get in the tent."

Georgie crouches and climbs through the flap. It isn't high enough for a person to stand easily, a small two-person tent, and besides she is too weary to stand, even to think and make a plan herself, so she sits on the sleeping bag with Freddy on the pillow and faces the entrance. Thomas beside her.

She can see the women's boots through the flaps, her tanned legs, the bottom of her shorts and Oona from the waist down.

"Just sit down," the woman calls. "We've got some time here before we leave."

"What does that mean?" Thomas' voice reverberates. "Leave for where?"

"None of your business where you're going."

"Do you think she really has a gun?" he whispers to Georgie.

"Hush."

"She can't hear us over the sound of the

river," Thomas says.

Georgie shrugs.

"It's wise to believe what she says."

Outside, Oona is whimpering.

The woman is leaning through the flap.

"Is there a pig in here?" she asks. "The girl wants her pig."

Thomas picks Freddy up from Georgie's lap.

"Here," he says. "Freddy."

The woman reaches in and takes the pig.

"We'll hit the road in about half an hour," the woman says. "I got it together now and we'll be motoring pronto."

"What road?" Thomas whispers to Georgie.

"Maybe the road home," Georgie says.

"Does she scare you?"

"I don't know if she scares me, but we have found Oona. That's enough for me."

"Enough would be heading up the river to Roosevelt."

"But that is not happening, Thomas. Not yet."

He reaches in the back pocket of his shorts for his journal, leans against the pole of the tent and opens to the last page he wrote.

"What's happening in there," the woman calls into the tent. "What's that in your hands, kid?"

"It's my journal," Thomas says. "I am writing a journal about this trip."

"That's nice. That's very nice writing a journal. I should do that," she says. "My name by the way is Linda in case you're planning to put me in the journal."

Outside the tent, a sudden darkness and the figures through the flap move out of Georgie's view.

The woman is standing and Oona can no longer be seen.

The wind picks up, slapping the canvas tent.

"A storm?" Georgie calls to the woman.

There is no answer, but she can see her legs as high as her thighs, just below the shorts.

"What do you think?" Thomas asks.

"Either there's a cloud covering the sun and it will pass by, or a storm, or both." Georgie leans back to see more of the woman through the flap. Oona's legs are hanging in view so the woman must be holding her. No socks and her feet are muddy.

"What now?" Thomas asks.

Georgie is listening.

In the distance, far in the distance — thunder and a high gust whips through the pines above them.

It is a storm.

A sudden hammering of rain and the woman takes cover in the tent, dropping to the ground, Oona in her arms.

"No funny business," she says. "This storm will be done in a flash and then I'll go on with my plan. I know all about the weather in Missing Lake."

She is sitting on the tent flap, holding the child, her left arm around Oona's torso, her hand on the pocket holding the gun.

The tent small, damp, suddenly cold, fills with too sweet a smell — maybe cheap perfume or the stank odor of the woman's body. Too strong for a small space.

Next to her, Thomas buries his face in his knees.

"Hello, Oona," Georgie says quietly.

Oona's eyes are wide, as if she is holding them open.

"You know the rules here," the woman says.

Even in the semidarkness of the tent, she is so close that Georgie can see her heavy-lidded eyes, the slight tremor in her arm, a look of desperation on her face. Her lips tremble from nerves.

"I was at the bar at Blake's Lodge Monday night with my boyfriend and saw all you guys and I saw the child."

She rearranges Oona on her lap.

"The next morning while you were paddling to Missing Lake, I came here with my wheelbarrow and left it as a sign that someone had been here and it was me and I was going to take the child." She lifts her arm that has been concealing the gun and brushes the hair out of her eyes. "I leave signs. Get it?"

Georgie nods although she does not *get it.*

"I don't get it," Thomas says.

"My father made me that wheelbarrow when I was a little girl and I keep it on my front porch where I live in the Shallows." She takes a deep exasperated breath. "So now you understand?"

"I do," Georgie says speaking lightly as if nothing is of consequence.

She is vigilant, but somehow the urgency of the situation is vanishing.

The pelting rain hammers the canvas tent, but thunder no longer roars above them, and in her peripheral vision Georgie can see the woman's eyes beginning to close, then flapping open.

"I got here way before the sun rose and told the child I would hurt her if she screamed and I would have hurt her but she didn't scream."

She sits — her knees bent, her legs under her, Oona on her lap.

"I need a cigarette."

"I don't have one," Georgie says. "I don't smoke."

"A cigarette would calm me down," she says. "You surprised me coming up the path like you did. I heard someone behind me and stepped out of the forest and there you were coming up the path. I could have shot you then, but I didn't."

The rain diminishes to thin drops. Thunder in the far distance moving south, and the woman starts to stand, losing her balance.

"Shit."

She tries again, pulling herself up holding onto a tent pole sufficiently pliable to bend.

This time she gets halfway to standing and falls against the tent behind her.

"Forget it," she says to no one in particular. "I'm a little tired because I was up all night."

Outside, a cacophony of bird cries, the wind settles to a soft breeze, the sun through the flap shines a half circle of light into the tent.

"Everybody in Missing Lake knows about your father," the woman says. "It's the only famous thing that ever happened in this town where nothing happens, and we tell that story to our children."

"How do you tell the story?" Georgie asks.

"We say your father strangled your mother and went to jail and died."

"Do they say why he killed her?" Georgie asks.

"He wanted her dead is what they say."

She seems to be preparing to stand again, on one knee now.

"I don't tell that story to my children because I don't have any."

She pushes herself up slowly and finally she is standing, a little unsteady, Oona still in her arms.

"I'm going first and you follow me," she says.

Georgie gets up, waiting until the woman is outside, Thomas behind her.

Outside the tent, the day has turned suddenly bright and cloudless.

Georgie leans against a large rock, Thomas squatting on the ground beside her.

The woman is next to the tent and standing. Oona, her fingers splayed across her eyes, is in her arms.

"Heading to Camp Minnie HaHa now?" the woman asks.

Georgie hesitates.

"My children are already there," she says

finally, adding, to test the temper of the moment, "We're going to Minnie HaHa with Oona."

The woman shakes her head. "You are not going to take Oona," she says.

Oona uncovers her eyes, looking up at Georgie, and from somewhere deep inside her body, a high-pitched shriek.

Then silence.

The air is still.

The pines above them soundless, the sun even warm on Georgie's face.

Oona's eyes are closed.

The woman speaks into the quiet.

"You can call me by my name."

"Linda," Georgie repeats, as if her name spoken aloud might settle the woman's nerves.

There is a long pause.

It appears from the short distance between them that tears are spilling into the corner of Linda's red-rimmed eyes.

"When I was younger," she says. "I had a little girl and my little girl died."

Georgie's throat tightens as if to close without warning. She pushes herself off the rock.

In the last few years, something has changed in Georgie's response to her world, as if here and there a missing synapse causes a commotion in her brain and she has to catch an emotion on the fly.

Now, the summer of Rose.

"I am so sorry," she says to the woman, Linda. "I don't know what to say but that."

She walks away from the tent, up the slight hill to the place where she has chosen to believe that her mother's body was discovered among the roots of an ancient oak tree.

"Where are you going?"

"Just up here before we leave for camp."

She kneels beside the tree, her legs damp with wet leaves.

Georgie called the girl Rose because in just that month of her eleventh year, she had gone from bud to bloom — trailing Georgie wherever she went among the Baos in Botswana. In this village scooped out of the jungle, she imitated the way Georgie folded the tops of her fingers together, resting her lips against them, the way she flung her hair out of her eyes and pinned it back in a comb although Rose's hair was kinky and not long. The way Georgie touched . . . talking with her hands, resting them briefly on an arm, a shoulder, a waist, gathering the community into her.

Woo was Rose's name for Georgie, and she breathed it into the air, her lips open and together as if to whistle — *wooooo* was the sound she made coming from the back of her throat.

They cooked together and walked together and carried water and built the fire in the evening and danced together. It was the summer after Georgie and Charley were married, Charley in Ann Arbor. Georgie overflowing with love took on Rose as her own.

Until one afternoon, late August, a storm — sitting with Rose in her hut, teaching her to make a pot out of mud, watching her fingers smooth the clay.

She thought she heard thunder.

Shhh, she said to Rose. Listening.

Thunder on such a day, hot, humid, but with a stiff breeze.

The sound louder and louder, coming in her direction not from the heavens but from the earth. She peered out of the hut, and there were the men, bare-chested, not running, loping, spread, maybe ten across the wide center of the village turned brown with the sun, their bare feet slapping the hard ground, and out of their mouths, their throats, their bellies, came a sound like a growl, like a pack of dogs.

In unison. A loud unmistakable sound of grief.

From Rose, barely audible, atonal, without

a breath — a long high-pitched whine.

An answering call to her people.

The men stopped in front of the tent, the whole crowd of them saying her name, the name she had been given by the tribe.

Not Rose.

She stood, handed the half-formed pot to Georgie without looking her in the eye, her chin up, her back straight, and she walked through the middle line of the band of men, disappearing beyond them.

Inside the hut, Georgie sat on her haunches, water on her fingers, smoothing the pot until there were no longer protrusions of clay, no cracks. Only a perfect circle the size of a grapefruit hollowed out to hold water once it was baked in the sun.

She did not go out of the hut to the communal meal that evening. Rather she sat cross-legged on the dirt floor writing a letter in her notebook to Charley. Not one that she would send but one to read when she got back to the states in late August.

Dear Charley,

When I arrived at the village July 29, I was homesick. I have never belonged and now I have you and you are home but thousands of miles away.

Coming here where I know the people

274

and they trust me — a sudden sickness for home. I laid claim to this young girl and made up my own name for her, which was Rose, and made her believe that I was indispensable to her — when in truth she was indispensable to me.

Now sitting alone in my hut writing you to the rhythm of voices just outside, I understand how things go here for the rest of the summer. How they will go summers in the future. Slowly . . . and I will have to start my work all over again as if as a stranger.

I am someone they no longer trust, who took from them what did not belong to me.

Always, G

Why now? Why suddenly Rose, who must be in her late fifties if she is still alive, and Georgie hasn't thought of her for years.

Likely Rose *never* thought of Georgie.

After all, it was nothing. Just a week or two of a tiny love affair.

"Thomas?" she calls, stepping away from the rooted bed of her mother's death. "Help me pack up."

She walks down the hill to where the last canoe is anchored, unties the rope and turns the canoe right side up.

Thomas is taking down the tent, folding it, tying the rope to contain it. Together they roll the sleeping bags, zip the backpacks and carry the equipment to the bank, packing it in the center of the canoe, leaving room for Oona, who will be in the bow between Georgie's legs.

They don't talk.

Above them, the woman Linda stands holding Oona's hand. She has taken off her boots and rocks back and forth in bare feet.

Thunder in the far distance, the light dimming, and Thomas looks up.

A moving cloud covers the sun.

Georgie finishes loading in the gear and stands, stretching her back.

"Getting chilly," she says.

"I hope it's not going to rain."

The woman makes her way down the hill, walking slowly toward the river where Thomas is pushing the canoe into the water, holding on to the rope.

"You know Roosevelt McCrary, don't you," Linda, says.

"I have never met him," Georgie says. "But I will."

"He told me he was meeting you," she says. "I know him too ever since I was born and I am forty-two."

Up close and in the sun, she is ravaged, but her wide-set brown eyes, strong bones and straight back suggest another woman than this one.

Georgie reaches out her hand and Oona takes it and climbs into the bow.

Linda does not resist.

"Storms come in and out," she says. "Sometimes two or three short ones a day, so if that thunder you are hearing moves much closer and the day gets darker, paddle the boat to the bank and tie up and wait it out," Linda says. "Don't stay on the water."

"Thank you," Georgie says.

"I was lying about the gun," Linda says, and turns away from the bank. "I told you I had a gun, but I do not."

Georgie follows her.

"Wait," she calls. "I want to say goodbye."

The woman turns, standing very straight, something courageous about the way she looks at Georgie.

"Thank you," Georgie says. "Thank you for taking care of Oona."

And then, without a thought, she wraps her arms around the woman's shoulders.

"I am so sorry," she says.

Linda starts to speak but stops herself, shaking her head.

Georgie can feel Linda watching her walk

down the bank to the river.

"Linda McCrary," the woman calls, and Georgie hears *Linda McCrary* clearly, but she does not turn around.

At the bank, Georgie wades into the shallows of the river and climbs into the bow, Oona between her knees.

"Ready," she calls to Thomas, and picks up the paddle and does not look back.

From the Memoir of Thomas Davies

(FOR PUBLICATION)

Strange the way you can walk the surface of the earth, one step at a time with a clear destination in mind, and suddenly the dependable planet opens without warning and drops you into a black hole.

My father died by inches.

I do not believe in heaven and if I did, I'd *know* we will all be fine and so will Oona. No problem because we will be in heaven and get to see each other sooner or later.

Honestly.

People believe this kind of thing.

What I do believe in is reincarnation. Or thermodynamics, which is sort of the same thing if you want it to be. Even my father, Dr. Richard Davies who was a scientist, told me when he was dying that, in fact, his death would not be the *end* of him. He told me that the first law of thermodynamics says that the total amount of energy in a closed system (like the body of a man is a closed system) cannot be created or destroyed although it can be changed from one form to another.

So that is what I believe.

I think of Georgie as young although she isn't young. But the total amount of energy in her closed system of energy is so electric that I can feel it.

We were sitting at breakfast one morning after I moved with my mother from our apartment in Chicago to live with Georgie and anyone else who happened to knock at the front door to ask for a place to live.

Georgie would open the door wide and say: *Welcome. Come in. There's a bedroom free on the third floor with a private bath. No worries if you're a serial killer. Or a prostitute. Or have a jail record. Everyone is welcome at the Home for the Incurables.*

I hated it.

I had moved from a small, quiet apartment in Chicago to this *hotel of lost souls* — that's what my mother calls it.

"But it's not lost souls, just people who are looking for a home" is what Georgie says. "And I give them one. Why not?"

I tend to agree with her now.

Why not?

It makes them happy and except for the garlic in the refrigerator, it makes me happy to come home from school and know that in the house, there will eight, nine, ten people who know me at least a little, who say "Hello, Thomas" and "How was school?" and "Do you have a soccer game this weekend?"

Once even, Mr. Adlerhouse gave me a signed copy of *The Odyssey.*

"Signed by whom?" Uncle Nicolas asked.

"Homer," I said, opening the book to the title page.

"To Thomas Davies, Good Luck and God-speed and for goodness sakes, don't leave home like I did. With love and admiration, Homer."

That's the kind of person who comes to live with us because of Georgie.

They pay attention because we all live in the same house.

But this particular morning was right after I moved to Washington and I was unhappy about everything — about the city, the plates at dinner, the living room, my bedroom with a round window overlooking the street, the school, the kids that went to the school, the dreadful teachers, the cats, six of them floating around my feet, the flowers all over the house in vases and teapots and mugs, the smell of cookies baking, the light coming in the living room from the west.

Everything that was not Chicago.

Georgie had made scrambled eggs and bacon and her own blueberry muffins, and I was sitting at the table looking at breakfast in front of me and out of the blue, I swiped my arm across the table, and the plate with breakfast slammed to the floor, scattering the eggs, shattering the plate.

Georgie did not even turn around from the dishwasher which she was loading.

"I hate eggs," I said. "Especially yours, which are mushy."

I grabbed my backback, put it over my shoulder, kicked the eggs and broken plate out of my way and headed out the back door feeling better than I had felt for a long time.

Georgie was home when I got back from school, so it must have been a Friday when she didn't have to teach and was working in the living room, which she likes to do, her feet on the coffee table, a computer on her lap, Beethoven's piano sonatas playing, always the same ones.

"Why don't you have your own office?" I asked when I arrived, crabby again once I walked through the front door.

"This is my office," she said.

"It's the living room," I said. "In most families the living room is where people live, not where they work."

"I like to be in the middle of my home," she said. "So I'm here when everyone comes back."

For a long time after my father died, I was not a nice person.

"Who says we *want* you to be here?" I asked her.

That's the kind of talking I used to do, and honest to God, Georgie never took me to the mat for it. Not because she is so patient. She isn't really patient at all.

"*I* want to be here" is what she said.

That's all she said and went on pecking at her computer without looking up.

Later that night, after dinner, after the boarders had gone upstairs to their own rooms and my mother was in her room and maybe Venus in hers or maybe sleeping with whatever boyfriend happened to invite her to spend the night, Georgie in the kitchen, drinking tea with honey and dark chocolate, which she did every night, I came in the room and asked for tea.

"Sure," she said, putting on the water.

I remember it was a hot night, the lights in the kitchen were on the dimmer. One of the cats, a long-haired gray one with a growly face, was sticking his paw in the honey jar without correction — music on the Bose, always music on the Bose — and I sat down across from Georgie, seeing her for the first time that I can remember, actually *seeing* her as beautiful.

Somehow, seeing her like that made me feel visible.

The night before we left Washington to come to Missing Lake, Wisconsin, there were fights on the telephone with Georgie and Uncle Nicolas, with Georgie and Nicolas' wife, Olivia, who is appearing at the Folger Theatre as Desdemona, with my mother who said she was coming down with something like flu and maybe it would be better if she stayed at home and Georgie went to Missing Lake with me and Venus.

"No, that isn't what is happening," Georgie said. "We are all going to Camp Minnie HaHa tomorrow morning as planned."

I was in the kitchen watching the steady rain roll across our windows, thinking of Annie Bayly in seventh grade with her long chestnut-colored hair (I'm not sure that's the color of her hair, but I like the sound of it) and gigantic blue eyes looking directly at me, unflinching — sort of chilly eyes and beguiling (I like the sound of that too), and she has one of those long, floaty bodies that seem to be tumbling through the air.

I am in love with her.

"Are we going or not?" I asked when Georgie put the phone down.

"Of course we're going."

I was suddenly a little nervous about this trip. I didn't like the fact that my mother had decided at the last moment to pretend to have a cold and thought nevertheless that it was perfectly alright for *me* to go with Georgie.

I've had enough trouble to wonder about life, to consider how to live it the way I want to live it without disaster or failure or disappointment or regret.

And something else.

Georgie has this way of making everything *seem* possible. But everything isn't possible.

Uncle Nicolas says this all the time.

Not possible.

That worries me.

Not the impossibility but the possibility. How can you believe something will come to be and at the same time with the same mind and the same heart understand that it might not come to be at all. How can two contradictory ideas exist in one small white mass of brain with little roads to everywhere inside the skull. But no way out.

I slid into a chair at the kitchen table beside her.

"I'm wondering," I began as she packed up her books in her tote and turned on the water for tea. "We are going on a trip and on this trip you think we are going to discover something about your father's innocence. But maybe we won't. Maybe we'll fail. Maybe Roosevelt is not who he says he is. Maybe your father did kill your mother. Maybe you discover nothing at all but disappointment."

"If I didn't believe I was going to discover *something,* then I wouldn't go," she said.

"So the truth of what happened with your father doesn't matter?" I said.

"It matters, but what is more important is the trip itself — believing that I will find something but knowing that I may not," she said.

■ ■ ■ ■

Missing Lake

■ ■ ■ ■

June 17, 1941

WILLIAM

The tent flap was open and in the distance, William could see a circle of light meandering across the landscape in his direction.

James.

He lifted his hand from Josie's, folded his arms across his chest and watched as the outline of a figure moved toward his tent.

Only James Willow would be up this late wandering the campsite — a surprising boldness in a young man timid by nature as if *he* were the one in charge, free to peer into the tent where William could possibly be sleeping. Or Josephine. Or they could be sleeping together.

Now that *was a joke!* William thought.

Besides, what did James know of the lives of adults — a boy really. A smart and capable boy but with no sense of intimate lives, no instinct for the complexities between men and women behind closed doors or tent flaps, as if what happened between them were all a fairy tale and James an instrument of dreams.

William heard his footsteps now sliding along the damp ground cover, light arriving in a splash through the tent flap spreading across Josie who was lying on her back and William, his head propped by blankets, looking straight into its brightness.

"James?"

"Yes, William. I was just checking. I wanted to make sure."

"Make sure of what?"

"That you're settled. I heard a terrible sound in the woods."

"You actually heard something besides the light wind?"

"I did. Minutes ago."

"There was no sound whatever in the woods, James," Josie said. "Just your invasive curiosity about our lives."

"I'm sure you're right. No sound," James said breathlessly. "But I'm a little agitated. Something about the night, William. I'm sorry to disturb you."

"I was disturbed before you arrived," William said.

He watched James move away, heard his footsteps behind their tent as he went up the hill and toward the tree line where his own tent was pitched.

And then the trace of light was gone, the sound of footsteps.

"I dislike him," Josephine said. "I cannot help myself."

"I know you do." William assumed a gentle tone of voice.

"He is in love with you," she said. "Every summer, the same thing. James Willow panting after you like a sick puppy."

There was a sudden heat in William's body. A rush of blood.

It angered him to think that Josie was right.

"You have that way with men and women," Josie said in a voice loud enough to carry to the tree line. "They want to be with you."

William stretched, raising his arms above his head and down, consciously down, letting his hand drop once again on Josie's, drop gently, barely a weight on her skin.

"I would like to be with *you.*"

She was quiet then, her free arm resting across her forehead.

"I don't really believe you, William," she said in a near whisper. "Here we are in Missing Lake, Wisconsin. A homosexual and two Negroes camping with us in this remote wood beside an angry river. A test of fate."

"And a Jew."

"Yes." Her voice less accusatory than resigned. "A Jew."

He looked over at his wife. Enough light from the stars slipping through the tent flap to see her face clearly, even the flat blankness of her eyes.

"Don't do anything to hurt me," she said quickly.

"Why would I do anything to hurt you, Josie?"

"I don't know." She turned her head slightly toward him. "Sometimes I am afraid. You are an angry man."

He lay very still.

Perhaps.

Perhaps he was an angry man.

He had a temper. He had always had a temper.

High-spirited, his mother said. But, his father insisted his temper was unacceptable and punished him for it — occasionally with a belt.

William was born with a temper, his mother would say in argument with his father. *Like brown eyes or long legs — what to do?*

His father would shake his head.

Brown eyes and long legs — you cannot cut them off. But a temper you can control.

As a boy, he had incidents of rage. When

going about his ordinary life in the village, something would upset him. Something unexpected.

He remembered one particular spring morning when he was ten or eleven walking with his father to synagogue. His father was talking about the meaning of Passover, and William asked him to please not speak any longer about the goodness or the courage or the long suffering of the Jews because it made him angry.

"It should make you proud," his father said.

"But it doesn't make me proud," William said. "It makes me angry."

And drawing his hands into a fist, he hit the trunk of a tree until his hands were bloody while his father, the doctor, stood calmly in attendance, his own hands clasped behind his back.

"Do you know *why* it makes you angry?" his father asked.

William was sobbing.

"I am crying with fury," he said. "You will never understand."

"I will probably understand," his father said, taking William's bloody hand in his own. "Do *you* understand?"

They were walking to the synagogue at the far end of the road, walking past the cottages of the other Jewish families on their way to synagogue, the men and boys spilling out of the houses, waving, calling out to the Geringas, Dr. Geringas and his son William,

"Good morning, good morning."

Tears of anger rushed down William's cheeks. He averted his face.

"I don't like victims," he said to his father as they walked up the steps to synagogue.

"I didn't say we were victims, William. We are *not* victims."

"You said long suffering. I don't like long suffering."

"Maybe you aren't ready for this conversation."

"I *am* ready for this conversation, Papa. If someone hits me, I will hit him back. I will break his nose," he said. "Maybe I will even kill him."

His father dropped his hand.

Later he told his father he was sorry. Deeply sorry. He understood and was proud to be a Jew.

And that was true.

But sometimes when he felt powerless, he could not help himself. He wanted to be a god of war.

"There are many ways to be a god of war," his father said to him. "Many better ways to fight than that."

William lay quietly concentrating on the stillness of his mind, the weight of his body on the damp earth. He did not allow himself to think of his village, where his father at this very moment was possibly in the hands of the Nazis. Or dead.

Perhaps he should be thinking about Clementine. Her long legs and straight back, her graceful hands and slender fingers — the way she cocked her head.

But such imagined thinking was not possible with Josephine beside him erupting with contempt.

For him. Even for herself.

Since they left Chicago, his body had been on fire.

He closed his eyes, took hold of himself, flaccid between his legs.

"I'll be back in a moment," he said, too agitated to lie next to her.

"Where are you going?"

"I have to pee," he said.

"You'll be back?"

"I'll be back, of course."

Pulling up his trousers, he ducked out of the tent, tripping first over the low folding chair where Josie had been sitting and then on the extra rope for anchoring the canoes.

He folded the chair, tossed the rope beside it and walked toward the wood.

He should have brought a flashlight to go into the darkness, he thought, but he would pee on the edge of the forest.

Afterward he leaned against a full-grown pine, heavy with branches, and waited to feel his temper dissipate, descending the tunnel of his body and out through his feet. That was the way he thought about anger, as an electrical current shooting through his body and out.

He *needed* to make love to Josephine Grove, to lay claim to her as his wife.

Closing his eyes, breathing the damp air deep into his lungs, he was beginning to feel the possibility.

William was the only Geringas son still in Lithuania in January 1930, when he left for New York. His brothers had been in England for two years and his parents, both anxious to keep him close and also to push him out, had made arrangements with his father's brother Irving Geringas, now Grove, a physician in Washington, D.C.

"Finish your studies and come home," his mother had said to him. "Don't find an American wife. She would never be happy here."

"Maybe I won't come back," William said. "Just stay in America with my American wife."

"Oh, you will be back," his mother said, giving him a slap on his behind for emphasis.

"Or maybe you won't," his father said. "Irving didn't come home. He has never been home. Once he became a doctor, he stayed and that could happen to you."

They were walking through town together as they often did. His father liked to walk, and he liked to talk beyond the hearing of his wife, who talked often but seldom walked except to the market.

"As for an American wife, she should be Jewish." He shrugged. "For company. You will need company."

In three years, January 1933, Hitler would be appointed chancellor of Germany, as the leader of the Nazi Party hostile to the democratic policies of the Weimer Republic, advocating extreme nationalism, promoting anti-Semitism.

But even in 1930, thinking men in Lithuania like Dr. Geringas were aware of underlying dangers for the Jews.

"Consider carefully what you do and say in America. It is a democratic country, but there are feelings everywhere," his father said to him on this long walk.

William listened but with half an ear.

"There is a human desire to be better than others, to stay on top, to push others out. A need to have a tribe and stay with your own people. It is the way we human animals are."

At the train station when William was leaving Vilnius, his parents were on the platform, his mother, his small plump mother, stood very straight and did not weep.

His father took his face in his hands and kissed him on the lips.

"Goodbye, my son," he said. "Be who you are wherever you may go, and watch that temper that it doesn't run away with you."

The last he heard his father's voice.

Many letters. Many, many letters and cards and photographs. But not his voice.

It came to William as he walked through the darkness under the high pines whining in the light wind and ducked into the tent where Josephine was lying, that he would never hear his father's voice again.

■ ■ ■ ■

THE BONE RIVER

■ ■ ■ ■

June 18, 2008

GEORGIANNA

Thomas leans back, his paddle at an angle, guiding the canoe to the left into the middle of the river, headed north. A swell. They feel it hammer the hull of the canoe.

In the bow, Oona is pressed between Georgie's outstretched legs, Freddy in her lap. She wraps her arms around her grandmother's calves and chatters.

"I was sleeping," she is telling Georgie, "and then I was having a dream and the dream turned into these arms all around me, lifting me up and the person named Linda who smelled just terrible was holding me and I squiggled and squiggled and she didn't even drop me — she had very strong arms wrapped around my arms and I kicked her and she flung my legs out away from her so I couldn't really kick . . .

"And then she stopped holding me too tight and told me she had asked you, my grandmother, could she take me to see her house where she had lots of toys that had belonged to her own little girl and you said okay."

She took a deep breath, resting her head against Georgie's knee.

"She did not hurt me."

"Were you worried when she said she had a gun?"

"She didn't tell me she had a gun, and then when you and Thomas came, she told *you* she had a gun and it turned out to be not a gun at all. And then you hugged her."

"I did hug her."

"So you were friends."

"We did not know each other before this morning."

"So you didn't give her permission to take me?"

"I would not have allowed her to take you to her house, no matter about the toys," Georgie says. "But yes, I hugged her."

Before Georgie can think of how to tell Oona about the sudden rush of love for Linda that had overtaken her, the child has fallen asleep, her chin resting on the orange life preserver.

No one, not even Thomas who is too young, or any of her children, except possibly Venus, would understand.

■ ■ ■ ■

The day is pure and glorious, a deep blue cloudless afternoon, the sun almost hot on Georgie's shoulders. *Dip swing, dip swing, dip swing* — she is conscious that on the return swing her paddle just grazes the top of the quiet river. Her body from the waist up is straight, so she is pulling the paddle in the *dip* deep enough for a long pull, precise along the hull.

The ordered repetition settles her.

Oona, in a deep rag-doll sleep, is humming.

Georgie feels a kind of ease in her body like relief but more buoyant than relief. As if she is emerging from old skin discarded in the pine wood. As if the warm tears filling the corners of her eyes, rolling down her cheeks, were extract — the essence of a new and extra hour extending the day, delaying the fall of night.

"Are you thinking about Roosevelt?" Thomas calls from the stern.

But Georgie doesn't hear him — the splash of water off the paddles, the light wind, the distance between them in the canoe — she doesn't wish to interrupt this moment, this unfamiliar moment of . . . is it

303

happiness?

And does happiness, pure happiness like this, only come at the expense of almost losing everything that matters?

Or is happiness *itself* just a visitor that might at any moment fly away or, unattended, remain but briefly, not always recognized for what it is.

Losing and finding Oona was at the center.

Losing and finding.

Is this what it means to be truly alive, so the past is never past and the present ever expanding its square footage to accommodate tomorrow in the same fluid space?

In a matter of an hour or so, she will see Roosevelt. He'll be on the dock. There must be a dock. Waiting for her, looking out over the river, his heart full, his thoughts crowded with imaginings of Georgianna.

They will walk together along the paths to the cabins, to the lodge, to the campfire, into the woods. Talking and talking. He will tell her everything he knows and she will listen.

Suppose he says that her father did *not* kill her mother. That actually it was James Willow and then James went off to die in a plane in the Second World War.

Or possibly Roosevelt tells Georgie that her father *did* kill her mother for a reason or no reason at all. In a fit of rage. A moment of anguish for his own and real family.

Would knowing have made a difference to her life? Would it now?

Whatever happened to the urgency of this trip to Minnie HaHa.

Or has she already discovered what she had hoped to find but has yet to find the language to name it.

"Georgie," Thomas calls out, shouting over the sounds of the river. "Look! Look up!"

Georgie lifts her head.

Above, a bright, clear afternoon sky. Ahead, a wide black stripe descending on the horizon as they move toward what is most certainly a storm.

A summer storm moving in their direction, a light rain advancing the storm, skimming Georgie's skin. The air is quite suddenly cool.

The swells under the boat lift to waves from the bowels of the river, splashing against the hull, rocking the canoe.

The promised storm. Sometimes two or three a day, the woman Linda said.

Oona raises her head.

"It's raining all over my arms."

"Turn in," Georgie calls out to Thomas. "Head us to the left bank."

"Lean forward," Thomas calls back. "Paddle as hard as you can."

And then their voices cannot be heard above the wind.

Georgie pushes Oona to the bottom of the canoe: "Stay down," she says and, resting on her knees, she spreads her body forward, stretching over starboard, her torso on the gunnel, forcing the paddle into the water as far as she can reach. She holds tight to the bottom of the shaft where it meets the paddle — *dip, swing* — the swing nearly impossible against the wind.

But they *are* moving left toward the bank.

Georgie is counting. "One," she says aloud. Two. And Three. And Four. And Five. On and on and on to a hundred. Five hundred will get them to the bank if the wind would only cease its pounding, pushing them back, each time they move forward in the current.

One stroke forward, one stroke back.

The canoe is turning in a half circle, heading south in the direction of Missing Lake. The bank to which they have been headed is now on the right of their boat and they are moving left.

The banks on either side of the river which had seemed to be a short distance apart are separated now by miles. Georgie cannot even see through the film of weather to the other side.

She shouts *right* and the sound reverberates through the wind like a growl in her ear.

But Thomas cannot hear her.

She tries to put her paddle in the water directly away from her body, pulling the water toward the boat, but the storm is too strong. Her body cannot unfold to upright in the wind, and she falls against the side of the canoe now going in circles, rocking back and forth, shipping water.

She rights herself, leans forward, tries to submerge her paddle in the river, but she cannot move it against a wind that has the strength to whip the paddle into the air, out of her hands, and it is gone.

They are going to capsize.

She pulls Oona up from the floor of the canoe, secures her hand on the straps of Oona's life preserver so she can't slip away.

"We're going to tip over into the river and I'm holding on to you so you won't go under and I'm in my life preserver and I won't go under so we're going to be just fine."

She speaks in Oona's ear.

The boat rolls, ships more water into their laps, dipping backward. The stern must be under water now, the bow up and Georgie is in the river, the straps of Oona's life preserver tight in her fist.

"Keep your head up above the waves," she shouts at Oona, stretching her own neck, her head tilted back, the river splashing over her face.

A dim flicker of light skips across the top of the waves.

The wind on her skin is icy cold, the rain falling in sheets straight down from the heavens. She cannot keep her eyes open.

"Head up!" she shouts at Oona again and again.

And then below the surface of the water, where Georgie's legs hang twisted by the current, something is happening. Some settlement, as if in the river's depths at the muddy bottom a switch has been turned to OFF.

The sheets of rain move behind them. She can even feel their departure.

A battalion in lock step pushed south by the wind.

There's a brief drizzle, the waves relax to gentle swells, the sky reflected on the water brightens.

And then the sun.

Treading water, Oona beside her, Georgie makes her way to the bank ahead through the current gone almost still.

Thomas is on his back, half-sitting, his elbows ballast as Georgie, gripping the strap of Oona's life preserver, reaches the bank.

He sits up when he sees them.

"Are you guys okay?" he asks.

"Well . . . yes. I think we are."

"Pretty terrifying," he says as Georgie makes her way up the muddy bank with Oona.

Georgie takes off the life preservers and lays them on the bank to dry.

"How long do you think that took?" she asks, sitting beside Thomas.

"The storm? Ten minutes?"

"Not even," Georgie says. "It went by like a freight train."

She is lying on her back now, her arms over her head looking up at the sun shifting west.

And then she remembers.

"The canoe!"

"You climbed up the bank right beside it and you didn't even notice?"

She lifts her head.

Anchored to a tree, the canoe rocks in the

light breeze. Georgie's paddle is gone, but the paddle Thomas was using is under the seat in the stern of the canoe, where he must have stored it when he went into the river.

"Only one paddle," Thomas says. "But I can get us to Minnie HaHa with one paddle."

"Did we almost die?" Oona asks.

She has taken off her wet clothes, now naked, her arms spread in a V up to the sky.

"We did *not* almost die," Georgie says. "The storm went away quickly and now we're safe."

"You weren't freaked out?" Thomas asks.

"I didn't have time."

"Are you ready to head to the camp now?"

Georgie stands, stretches, shakes the water out of her hair.

"Put something on, Oona," she says. "Maybe just your underpants."

"They're wet."

"Put on your wet underpants."

Thomas picks up his backpack, one strap around his shoulder.

"What happened with you and that woman, Linda?" he asks.

"It just happened."

"Completely weird," he says. "I looked over and you're hugging her as if the two of you are the best of friends, and I thought as

I usually think with grown-ups, you make no sense at all."

"I don't know what came over me," Georgie says, making her way down the bank to the canoe. "She broke my heart."

They shake the life preservers, buckle them and push the canoe off the bank. Walking against the tide through the shallow water, they pour themselves into the boat — first Georgie with Oona, careful not to tip the canoe.

The boat moves quietly up the middle of the river into an afternoon bright enough to see the land curve in the distance, opening to a deep cove.

Georgie, on the ribbed bottom of the canoe with Oona between her legs, leans against the seat.

"Now Roosevelt!" she says.

They move easily into the curve of land circling to a cove. At the end, a half-circle and a dock jutting into the river. Squinting into the sun, Georgie makes out a hill, a rise of land dotted with small square structures, probably cabins and a long rectangle of a lodge.

Is this familiar, Georgie wonders, thinking she remembers exactly this picture, or is it

the picture on all the postcards from Roosevelt that she has received since December
zipped up now in her backpack.

People are standing on the dock, small
spots of color sprinkle the horizon.

Oona stretches, her arms high, and she
rolls toward Georgie.

"Guess what?" she says.

"Well?" Georgie asks.

"I'm here."

"I see you here right in front of me looking just like yourself."

"And where *is* here?"

"*Here* is the Bone River and Thomas is
paddling our canoe up the river to Camp
Minnie HaHa and soon we'll be *there*."

"What is going to be at Camp Minnie
HaHa when we get there?"

"Your father, your brother, Aunt Rosie,
Aunt Venus. Roosevelt."

"I don't know Roosevelt."

"He is our friend whom we've never met."

"And will we just sit at a table while the
grown-ups talk and talk and talk like happens at your house?"

"You'll look around, go swimming, eat
dinner, meet Roosevelt and sleep over,"
Georgie says. "This is exactly the place
where I was going when I was four years
old, but I never arrived and now I will." She

312

rests her chin on the top of Oona's head. "With you!"

■ ■ ■ ■

CAMP
MINNIE HAHA

■ ■ ■ ■

June 18, 2008

ROOSEVELT

Roosevelt stands at the top of the hill above the dock, shadowed by a stand of pine. From the distance of the river, he fades into the woods, and in semidarkness he seems as wide as the stand of trees.

He is taller than Georgie has imagined, and still, as if painted onto the landscape. What appears to be a cane leans at an angle against his leg. A dog lies at his feet, her nose resting between her paws.

Thomas steers the canoe into shallow water, jumps out waving to his family on the dock.

"Oona is *here!*" he shouts, pulling the boat to shore.

Knee-deep in the river, Nicolas is waiting.

He lifts Oona out, into his arms, and buries his head in her chest, walking along the shoreline away from the family.

Rosie sits with Venus on the edge of the diving board, their legs dangling, their

317

shoulders touching in more intimate proximity than Georgie has seen them since they were girls.

"Oona?" Venus asks as Georgie climbs up to the dock. "Is she okay?"

"She is fine."

"Fine?" Rosie asks. "What happened?"

"Did she get lost?" Venus asks.

"Not lost exactly."

Georgie stands next to them, watching Nicolas walk in the river along the shoreline, holding Oona like an infant in his arms.

"So what happened?"

"It was . . . maybe a misunderstanding," Georgie says, wondering as she speaks how to tell the story about Linda. Why *misunderstanding* feels right in spirit if not in fact.

The woman — Linda — went into the tent and picked up a sleeping Oona and lied to her.

There was no misunderstanding, so *why* the need to excuse what happened?

Why am I not outraged? Georgie asks herself.

But she is not.

"Do you *know* what happened?" Rosie asks.

"Oona was taken out of her tent by a woman who is perhaps a little off."

"Kidnapped!" Venus says. "What does it

318

matter whether the woman was *off* or not?"

"I suppose literally it was kidnapping, but she had no ill intent except to take Oona to her house to play because she has a lot of toys she bought for her little girl who died."

"Honest to God, Georgie!" Venus throws up her arms. "People can tell you any terrible story and you believe them."

"Thomas and I discovered them, Linda and Oona, when we were on the path that leads to the town of Missing Lake," Georgie says, ignoring Venus. "They were on their way to Linda's cabin."

"Oh, Linda. Now she's Linda and you guys are friends?" Venus says.

"Georgie!" Rosie is standing now on the diving board. "In the middle of the darkness of night this woman is taking Oona to her house to play with toys? Is that what happened."

"Oona is fine," Georgie says, "and the woman is not a criminal, so why make so much about a happy ending."

"It's perfectly normal to abduct a child?" Venus asks.

"Nothing on this trip is perfectly normal."

Georgie runs her fingers through her wet hair, her combs lost at sea, her clothes wet, clinging to her skin.

"Ask Thomas what happened," Georgie

says. "Or Oona. Some things you have to see for yourself to understand."

Thomas pulls himself up to the dock holding the branch of a tree.

"This trip is turning out to be perfect," he says. "So far I have four stories to tell at Alice Deal in September. We even had a storm and the canoe capsized."

"Is that why Georgie looks like a drowned possum?" Venus asks.

"Are you okay?" Rosie asks, tousling his hair.

"I'm great!" Thomas says. "I'm going to meet Roosevelt, the only surviving witness to the murder of my grandmother."

"I need to catch my breath," Georgie says quietly — looking over at Roosevelt, who has not moved from his place on the hill, although from this angle, he appears to be tall and thin. Not wide.

"What do you two think?" she asks her daughters.

"He's reserved," Venus says. "I like him, but there's not much to know yet."

"He's accessible and dignified," Rosie says. "After two days with our family I was grateful to be with him. My blood pressure went down to zero."

"And I read his chart," Venus says. "Not perfect but pretty good. Born January 2,

1930. Kind and strong and stubborn. Something like that."

Georgie senses Roosevelt watching her walk along the bank beyond the dock and climb the slippery hill to the place where he is standing.

She is shivering — cold air on her wet clothes — shivering with nerves until she reaches the top of the hill and he takes her hand in his large rough hand and says, "Hello, Georgianna," in a voice so deep she can feel it in her body.

"Hello, Roosevelt McCrary," she says.

They both laugh — infectious, easy laugher as though they have known each other always.

Which they have, as Georgie imagines her world. Even before his letter and the postcards and the hours she has spent thinking about him, they have been in touch.

As she understands experience, they occupied the same space at a moment of great catastrophe.

They will always be in touch.

Handsome.

That pleases Georgie.

He has rich copper-colored skin unlined by so many years in the weather, strong bones, white curly hair partly hidden by a baseball cap. A quiet demeanor.

Just as she has imagined him.

At his feet, one paw crossed over her nose, is the black and white long-haired dog, her eyes half open.

"Mercy," he says. "My girl."

She can feel silence in the stillness of his body, as if the smell of his reserve is on his breath.

Cigarette breath, she notices.

"You're freezing," he says.

"We capsized on the river."

"I was afraid there might be one of those quick storms we get especially on the water."

He takes off the crew neck sweater he is wearing and puts it over her head, rolling up the sleeves.

"You look familiar," he says. "I've seen your photograph on the back of your books."

"You've read my books?"

"I have the one called *Home* about the tribe in Botswana."

She climbs up the short distance to the top of the mound.

"In the photograph on the book jacket, you have short hair."

He steps away from the tree.

"I was only thirty-nine in that photograph."

"But you look the same except your hair."

Georgie is seldom at a loss for conversation, but she is quiet now.

Perhaps if they walk into the camp together, away from her family, into the woods beyond the lodge, the weight of finally meeting after all of these months will disappear.

Maybe he has been thinking of her in the same way that she has been thinking of him.

He lives a solitary life.

Or not.

Linda McCrary.

Could she possibly be his wife?

Not likely, Georgie thinks not — too young for him. Too shattered. Nevertheless.

They walk up the hill to the lodge and stop.

"You found the child."

"She was on the path behind the campsite almost to the town of Missing Lake with a woman named Linda."

He stops, looking up as if to see the top of the stand of pines, his cane under his arm, his hands in the pockets of his jeans.

Considering.

"Do you know her?" Georgie asks.

They slip into the woods beyond the lodge onto a path to the cabins. The air is damp, the ground cover muddy, a light wind carries the smell of fungi and pine.

"I do know her," he says.

"She took Oona from the tent where she was sleeping before dawn, and we found them on the path just before we got to the town of Missing Lake," Georgie says. "Linda told me that she had a gun."

"She did not have a gun," Roosevelt says.

"She said later that she had lied," Georgie says.

"I should tell you about Linda."

"She told me she had a baby girl who died."

"The baby girl was stillborn and Linda has never recovered," he says. "It's . . ." He stops short of completing what he was going to say. "It's too complicated for tonight."

They walk along the path — Roosevelt just ahead, holding up low branches for Georgie to walk under. They come into a clearing, Mercy ambling between them.

The woods open to log cabins lined along the pine needle path.

"Named for Indian tribes," he tells her. "Chippewa and Cherokee and Iroquois and Navajo."

"Twelve cabins in all. Ten boys and a counselor to each cabin."

There are metal beds with thin striped mattresses, wooden flap windows held open in the good weather with a narrow board, a single electric light on the ceiling, pitched roof, a wooden porch.

Georgie peers in the screen door of Navajo . . .

Bleak.

The smell of damp wood, the weight of pine and darkness.

The sun is low in the sky, a heavy, bronze sun, and the light shimmers across the cabin logs, a splash of dark yellow on the door.

"This is the cabin where you lived with your parents."

Georgie walks up to the steps and stops.

"I haven't been here since I was three," she says.

"It's unchanged," Roosevelt kicks the mud off his boots. "New screens, the front door replaced, but otherwise the same."

She doesn't have a visual memory of camp, but when she thinks of Minnie HaHa, what she remembers is light and open air, rolling grassy hills and space.

Not how it is. Not how she has wished for it to be.

Too old and dank and cold.

Does sunlight ever filter through the trees or is the day as dark as night all summer long?

Here is the cabin pushed up against the forest in northern Wisconsin where she lived at the beginning of her life.

Happily?

What does she remember of happiness, or is there any definition to happiness when you're very young.

"Is it familiar?"

Roosevelt's warm voice fills the silence.

"It's . . . I don't know . . . but not exactly familiar to my memory of it."

What Georgie does have is a sense of returning to the long empty days of a northern summer sun in Michigan with her grandparents sitting in the living room, silent and together. Georgie on the rose velvet couch with a Nancy Drew mystery waiting for her life to begin.

"I seem to have imagined it better than it is."

Roosevelt goes up the steps, pushes open the screen door and holds it for her.

"You're disappointed?" he says.

"It's more like homesick for this place as I have always thought of it."

"That's the trouble," Roosevelt says. "We want to make our childhood better than it was. Why not?"

"But I'm not disappointed," she says, her arm brushing his woolly sweater. "Just surprised."

They step inside a small room with a dark blue couch and two deck chairs in need of new canvas covers. A fireplace, smelling of burned wood.

"It can be cold in summer," he says.

Two bedrooms, one very small.

"So I must have slept in the small one."

"I was told by the camp nurse — she was still here when I came — that you slept in the big bedroom with your mother and that your father slept in this small one alone."

"Maybe I was afraid by myself."

Georgie opens the door to the smaller bedroom and peers in.

She knows little of her parents' habits of being. All her grandmother had to say of their life together was that Josephine had never been depressed until she married William Grove.

Georgie closes the door to the small bedroom and checks the larger one where she would have slept with her mother, but she doesn't go in.

"I have a picture in my mind of walking in the dark to the latrine with my father," she says. "He let me carry my own flashlight and swing it around in circles in the sky. That's not the kind of thing you make up, is it?"

"I don't know about memory. It's tricky," he says. "When I think about what I remember, I seem to make the bad things worse and the good things better."

"Do you remember my mother?"

"I don't," he says. "I was only on the river the first day. After the police boat took your father, we left for home."

"Was there a lot of talk at the campsite after she was killed?"

"There was confusion and I was frightened. That I remember."

She follows Roosevelt back to the main room, leans against the cabin wall, her hands in the pockets of her shorts.

"Were you going to be a camper that summer?"

"I was hired by William to work on buildings and grounds."

"At eleven years old?"

"Young kids worked in 1941. Poor kids and black ones. But William had his eye out for me and wanted me out of the heat of Washington, D.C. So I came."

They are standing next to the fireplace, Georgie resting against the stone mantel.

"Why weren't you a camper?"

"There were no black campers," he says. "There still aren't more than a very few, from Chicago."

He leans down to brush off ash scattered on the rug, and when he stands, wiping the remaining ash on his jeans, he puts his hand on her arm for balance.

Georgie takes a breath, her pulse beating in her throat. She feels more urgent than awkward, which is what she had expected to feel.

So little time. Already it's late and they will be leaving Camp Minnie HaHa at dawn.

"Can you tell me about my father?" she asks. "Anything."

"I can," he says, his voice dropping as if there are others in the room besides Georgie he does not wish to hear. "I know the things you know about a person when you're young. I know he was strong and fit and took me places and told me stories," he says. "That was later, after he had moved to Ann Arbor and he'd come back to his uncle's to visit. Often, until he married."

"What kinds of stories?" Georgie asked,

"Wonderful stories about himself as a wild boy in Lithuania. Devilish, not bad."

He takes off his baseball cap, sticking it in his back pocket.

"That's all you remember?"

"All I remember but not all I know," he says. "Before Clementine died of cancer, she told me things about William that I had never heard."

"I never saw him again after that day when

he left with the police," Georgie says.

"Your grandparents never took you to the prison?"

"They did not," she says. "I understand why they didn't want me to see him again."

"They never talked to you about him?"

"Very little and mostly to remind me that he was a Jew."

"I do know what happened at the campsite," Roosevelt says. "At least the morning after your mother's body had been discovered."

"James Willow found her," Georgie says. "I read that."

"When the police arrived, William confessed," Roosevelt says. "I was sitting down the hill from your father's tent. He sat cross-legged outside his tent, sat very still waiting for the police to come. I couldn't take my eyes off him."

"The story of his confession was in the *Chicago Tribune*," Georgie says. "What I'm hoping you'll tell me is that his confession was not the real story. That possibly he was protecting someone else who *had* killed my mother."

Roosevelt shakes his head. "Certainly not James. He was a timid man who loved your father."

Georgie slipped into a chair across from

330

him, her feet on the low table.

"We have a list from the newspaper of the nine who were at Missing Lake. What about a stranger?" she asks.

"A stranger out of nowhere could not have found his way by land from the town of Missing Lake to the river. That path wasn't cut through until the sixties."

"No one among the nine at the campsite who might have had a reason?"

Roosevelt leans against the stone wall of the fireplace, his arms folded across his chest.

"There is information about William that I do know," Roosevelt says. "I went to see him before he died."

"You went to the prison?"

"Clem and I went out by train to Illinois — it took forever. We went on a bus to the prison and got off at this big cement building surrounded by a high fence and sat in metal chairs in a large room and they brought William out. We pulled the chairs up to a kind of counter and there was a screen between our faces, but we could hear him and see him."

"How did he look?"

"He was very ill. Normally he had dark skin, but his face had turned yellowish and bony. By the time we got back to Washington, Clem got a call from the prison to say that he had died. And we sat at the kitchen table and drank a lot of beer and cried our eyes out."

He brushes debris off the couch, cleans one of the deck chairs.

"My real father left when my mother got pregnant with me," he says. "So I was two years old when I met William."

Roosevelt takes a chair across from her.

"Am I making you anxious?" he asks.

"I'm anxious," Georgie says.

Butterflies in her stomach, her face hot for the chilly room, she is thinking what to ask Roosevelt, what to say.

Linda?

Or not.

"Almost seven," he says checking his watch, using the cane to get up from the chair. "It's time for dinner."

He puts out his hand to help her up from the couch.

"On the way back to the lodge I'll tell you about Linda."

He pushes open the screen door, slips his cane under his arm and Georgie follows him down the steps.

Dusk, the skies clear, the air light. The forest alive with sound.

He reaches over and for a moment rests

his large hand on her cold, wet head, and she feels his touch as heat through her body.

"I'm a mess," she says. "Because of that quick storm on the river we capsized."

"Lucky that's all that happened."

"It's been a lucky day," she says.

They walk slowly, Roosevelt preoccupied with his cane on the uneven path.

"You were going to tell me about Linda."

"I am," he says.

He takes her hand, and for what seems forever to Georgie, they walk in silence.

"Linda is mine," he says finally, his deep voice breaking on her name.

"What do you mean, she is yours?"

"My lonely mentally ill daughter, and she is the reason I have stayed through the godforsaken winters in northern Wisconsin. Because I must."

"You were married?"

"I was never married."

"Did Linda live here with you?"

"She did not. When her mother left Missing Lake, I took over watching out for her. She's unstable and promiscuous and has never had a long-term boyfriend except for Ray, the pharmacist in Missing Lake, who was the father of her baby. He stayed with her awhile after the baby girl and then he couldn't take it."

They walk side by side, their hands swinging.

"Hear the owl?" he asks.

"The hoot?"

"It's not dark and owls are only supposed to hoot in the dark, but that impertinent guy hoots whenever he damn well pleases."

"I know nothing about owls."

"They're my favorite of all the feathered creatures," he says. "Somehow they seem to have integrity and wisdom and reserve."

He puts his arm loosely around her shoulder.

"I especially like that they protect themselves from predators by drawing in their feathers and closing their eyes."

The pine forest path opens to a vista of the pale gray light of dusk, the lodge in the near distance.

"I'm not ready to go back to the lodge yet," she says, her voice thin, a familiar panic rising as if this moment is the last opportunity she will ever have with Roosevelt McCrary.

"There's something I need to ask just in case I don't have another chance," she says.

"I'll answer if I can."

"I don't understand how you happen to own this camp?"

"Because I'm not your father's son and

not white?"

"I guess that's what I mean."

"I own one-third. Thirty-three and one-third percent."

"But why?"

"When your father was director, the camp was owned by his uncle and two other doctors, who were friends. Your father died before his uncle and at your father's request his uncle left his one-third share to me. The other two present owners were grandsons of the original doctors, but they are not involved except financially."

"That's strange, isn't it?" Georgie asks. "You were Clementine's son and she was a cook in your uncle's house."

"It is less strange the more you discover."

Georgie rests her hand on his arm with the cane.

"Then tell me *everything* that you know."

"I will tell you everything I know," he says. "But later."

Roosevelt brushes thin strands of damp hair off her brow, out of her eyes, where they have fallen.

"Now dinner," he says.

Since Georgie can remember, she has been in a conscious retreat from sadness.

On a grief diet, she told Rosie — small portions of sadness carefully selected. Now she has a sense of danger, of something raw between them, as if Roosevelt will tell her something that might take the lid off of her Pandora's box and she will never be able to close it.

The ground is slippery with wet leaves, and they walk with care, Roosevelt's limp pronounced, her hand loosely in his as if an accident of proximity.

"Before Clem died in 1951, she told me that at your father's request Irving was leaving his interest in the camp to me," Roosevelt says. "So at twenty-one and at loose ends, I came here. A few months later Irving died and I have never left."

A riotous bird sound fills the air — a sudden chilly wind laced with raindrops.

"A storm?" she asks.

He shakes his head.

"Weather passing overhead. That's all."

She leans her head against his shoulder.

"So many things just don't make sense to me," she says.

"They will make sense," he says. "After dinner."

"At least I understand you were important to my father."

Georgie's heart is beating too fast, adrenaline rushing through her blood, her breath in short takes.

"What I want to know now, before we go into dinner, what I need to know is whether you believe my father killed my mother."

"He confessed to the police that he killed her."

Roosevelt puts her hand, which he is holding, gently in his pocket, his voice strong and certain, the sound of it reaching into the woods beyond Georgie.

"I've wanted to believe that he was protecting someone else," she says.

"Who would he have been protecting?"

"I don't know."

"We have no idea what went on between your parents except what your father confessed," Roosevelt says. "Not any one of us was there."

"But we can piece things together and either they add up or they don't, right?"

"There's nothing to piece together," he says gently. "Except to say that William Grove was a good and decent and courageous man, Georgianna. That I know."

"Then you believe that he killed her."

Roosevelt picks up fallen branches on the path, throwing them off to the side. Slow to respond.

"I do," he says finally.

"I was afraid that is what you'd say."

"And something else. That morning before the police arrived, Clementine walked up the hill to William's tent and spoke to him. *'You killed her William, didn't you?'*" she said.

"*'I did,'* he said. *'I did, I did, I did.'*"

"So that's all, I guess," Georgie says quietly. "All there is to say."

"Not all. Later, after dinner, I'll tell you."

They have come to the lodge and Roosevelt stops, lifts her hand and brings it to his lips.

"I leave early in the morning. I guess you know that," Georgie says.

"I do."

"Maybe you'll come to Washington and stay with us at the Home for the Incurables," Georgie says. "We always have an extra room."

They go through the swinging doors into the lodge, past the fireplace, into the dining area where Georgie's family is already sitting at a long table listening to Oona tell her story.

Thomas hops up.

"What do you know so far?" Thomas asks as Roosevelt heads into the kitchen.

"Nothing," Georgie says. "I know nothing."

"Do you think he's going to tell you?"

338

"I'm not certain that *he* knows anything," Georgie says.

"Of course he does."

"Thomas, cool your heels and come sit down with us. Leave Roosevelt alone," Nicolas says. "See what we can make of this visit. We're out of here at dawn for Chicago. The van will arrive at seven."

The table is long and the eight of them gather at one end, Roosevelt at the head. He opens a bottle of wine — serves the lemon chicken with wine and fresh green beans and biscuits.

"A fancy dinner for a boys' camp," Venus says.

"This is not how we eat when the boys are here," Roosevelt says. "This is the way Georgianna's father ate when he lived with his uncle in Washington, D.C., and my mother was the cook at Dr. Grove's house until she died."

He pours wine for himself and lifts his glass.

"To William Grove," he says. "And to Clementine, who taught me how to cook."

He reaches in his back pocket for a passport-size photograph of his mother that he passes around the table.

"I wanted you to see what she looked like," he says.

Summer in Washington — Clementine stands beside a magnolia tree in bloom — tall and slender like Roosevelt, unsmiling, her gaze direct, her arms behind her as she leans against the tree.

A faded color photograph, but still evident the pale pink of the magnolias, her high cheekbones and wide-set eyes, a whisper of a smile.

"Do you know that I got stolen in the middle of the night from my tent where I was sleeping with Freddy?" Oona presses the stuffed pink pig into Roosevelt's hand. "*This* is Freddy."

"Your father told me that you'd been stolen."

"This bad-smelling lady came into the tent and she told me that Georgie asked her to take me to her house where she had toys and dolls and candy surprises for me. She was pretty nice, but it was dark outside and she was carrying me and kept tripping and that made her say words like *fuck* which is a word I know from Jesse who is my brother."

"Her name is Linda," Thomas says.

"I know her name is Linda. She told us that," Oona says. "And Georgie hugged her. Now you and Linda are friends — right, Georgie."

"You hugged her?" Roosevelt asks Georgie.

"I did."

"Georgie is crazy," Nicolas says. "We've gotten used to it, but I feel the need to put her in perspective for you."

Roosevelt isn't listening.

He has made strawberry short cake for desert, the strawberries small and fresh, sweet biscuits and whipped cream.

He brings out another bottle of wine, leaning over to Georgie sitting beside him.

"Thank you, Georgianna," he says quietly, bending closer so she can hear him.

The night is cold and still. They clear the table and do the dishes — the clatter of plates against the counter, of glasses under the running water, Georgie leaning against the kitchen door listening to their laughter over nothing at all. Laughter — almost giddy laughter of relief that they are here. *Against all odds,* Nicolas says more than once.

"I thought it likely that we'd die. At least one of us," Nicolas says, Oona sitting on his shoulders.

Rosie slips into the sofa next to Thomas, resting against his shoulder.

"But we didn't die and now we're here

and it's kind of remarkable," she says.

Roosevelt lights a fire in the great room and Georgie's family sits on sofas around a dry wood blaze, their feet on the coffee table.

"Do you remember William?" Thomas asks.

"I do," Roosevelt says.

"I'm fascinated by him. I could hardly wait to meet you."

"What Thomas is fascinated by is murder," Nicolas says.

Roosevelt sits in a deck chair across from the sofa, his cane resting between his legs.

"What did he look like in the flesh?" Venus asks.

"Like Georgianna but tall. He had dark eyes and dark hair and strong bones. You've seen my photograph so you know."

"And what about Georgie's mother," Venus asks.

"I didn't know her," Roosevelt says. "All I heard after she died was that she had been beautiful and was depressed."

"Did anybody talk after she died?" Nicolas asks. "There must have been pandemonium at Missing Lake. Did your mother say something about it?"

"My mother didn't talk . . ." He hesitates. "She was silent when William was taken away by the police in a motorboat." His voice caught in his throat. "In handcuffs. William was in handcuffs."

"Is that surprising? He murdered his wife," Nicolas says.

"He did and sometimes a violent act may be that simple," Roosevelt says, his voice rising. "But this was not."

"What happened to make it not simple?" Thomas asks.

"I only know what happened to me that morning," he says. "I sat on a tarp near the river most of the time alone and eventually my mother sat down beside me. She asked me did I have my things together — we would be going home to Washington, D.C., as soon as a motorboat was free to take us to the lodge. There'd be a bus at the lodge to take us to Chicago.

"Then I asked, *Is everybody going home,* and Clementine said, *Just us,* and I asked, *How come just us,* and Clementine said, *We are only here because of William and I figure William is going to jail for the rest of his life.*"

"Because he killed her?" Venus asks.

"Yes because he killed her."

Roosevelt leans forward, rests his chin on his cane.

"That was all she said for days."

"Were you at the campsite when my

grandparents came to pick me up?" Georgie asks.

"They came by boat and your grandmother had on white gloves. Gloves in June. I remember that especially. I asked Clementine and she said something I can't remember, but I know that Dr. Irving Grove's wife did not wear white gloves in June."

"You never met my grandparents?"

"I didn't. I watched them. When they arrived, they went over to where you were sitting with the nurse — the only scene I really remember is that you screamed *'No!'* as your grandmother leaned down to take you from the nurse."

"And that was it?"

"You held your grandmother's white-gloved hand and hung your head down and walked straight by the tarp where I was sitting and climbed into the motorboat and left."

"What did you think of William?" Nicolas asks. "Or did you know him well enough to have an opinion."

"I knew him. I knew him very well," Roosevelt says, folding his hands behind his head, looking at Georgie. "He was a strong, decent, honorable man."

"Isn't that an odd description under the circumstances?" Nicolas asks.

Roosevelt's words are measured.

"I believe it's possible to be a decent man and in the heat of circumstance commit an unforgiveable crime. I *have* to think that."

He gets up and puts another log on the fire.

"Not a man likely to lose his temper and murder his wife?" Nicolas asks.

"Likely?"

Roosevelt adds another log and then another.

"People do all kinds of things in circumstances. According to my mother, he had a temper. He was known for that. And . . ." He hesitates, glancing at Georgie. "His wife was not an easy woman."

He folds his arms across his chest, standing at the head of the table — the room hushed.

"When Clementine was ill, the two of us had talks about her life. She told me that the Nazis were invading Lithuania, probably that very day, probably the village where William's family lived, and they were rounding up the Jews. You know that William was a Jew?"

"My grandmother wanted to be *sure* I knew," Georgie says.

"Georgie wants to believe her father was innocent," Nicolas says. "But it looks as if

345

that is *not* news you have to give her."

"The only proof I have is his confession," Roosevelt says, "if that's what you're asking."

"Maybe there isn't an answer," Venus says. "Maybe no one knows since no one was in the tent with him."

"Of course there's an answer," Thomas says. "Everything has some kind of answer."

"It can happen that when you're looking for something you can't locate, you discover something else," Roosevelt says. "Something more important."

"What might we find out?" Venus asks. "I'm all for new possibilities."

"Just an observation," Roosevelt says.

There is an ease about the evening, the company, the way the conversation floats over and around as if it were a part of all of them, as if they had always belonged together and to this place that none of them had ever even seen before except Georgie.

Roosevelt is ballast.

"It's odd, isn't it," Rosie says to Georgie when she kisses her goodnight, "as if we've always known him. And he isn't even chatty."

The rest of the family has gone upstairs in

the lodge to sleep. Including Thomas.

Only Georgie is left in the great room with Roosevelt watching the fire burn.

"Midnight," Roosevelt says. "I make a night check around the cabin area before I go to bed if you'd like to join me."

"I would. I will."

He hands her a flashlight, and they go out the screen door of the lodge, down the steps and into the darkness.

A perfect, clear, cold night brilliant with stars, a three-quarter moon.

"Easy to trip on roots," he says, and turns on the flashlight.

"I wish we *could* stay here longer," she says. "At least another day."

"The campers come tomorrow and you'll be glad not to be here."

They walk side by side along the path, close, Georgie brushing against him, her heart pumping, still a little breathless.

"Sweet night, wasn't it?" she asks.

"Better than I dreamed," he says.

They walk around the latrine, Roosevelt shining his flashlight into the woods.

"Have you ever had trouble here?"

"We have," he says. "Towns around here are poor, so people steal. Or sleep in the camp beds because they haven't got a place or had a fight with their wife. Not when the boys are here, but when I'm here alone."

"Do you worry in the wilderness?"

"I'm accustomed."

They walk in silence along the path from the latrine to the cabins, check them one by one, inside and out.

He stops by one.

"Listen."

Something is making a noise.

"Skunk."

He starts up the steps.

"Step back. Way back."

She slips into the stand of pine trunks.

"Hold on to Mercy's collar. She'll try to follow me."

He props open the screen door and steps in. Quiet at first except the sound of his voice speaking to the skunk and then in a matter of moments, the skunk saunters out, down the steps and meanders under the building.

"No smell?" she asks.

"They're not afraid of me."

"Why not you?"

"Because I'm not afraid of them," he says.

He joins her on the path to the next cabin and she leans lightly against him, eased by the safety of his presence. Something she has missed, this kind of safety.

A man who has the trust of skunks.

It makes her giggle how easily she is won over. Someday she will tell him *it was the skunk.*

"You were telling me about women in your life."

"Women." He has an easy laugh even more pleasing for his seriousness. "There are not a lot of women in Missing Lake. Hardly any now."

"So you're not going to answer me?"

"I am," he says.

He opens the door to the director's cabin and sits down on one of the deck chairs across from Georgie, who collapses on the couch.

"There were women in my life, but none I wished to marry. Including Linda's mother."

"You made Linda the red wheelbarrow. She told us."

"I made her a wheelbarrow to carry her dolls when she was a child. Now she walks down Main Street in Missing Lake with her toys in the wheelbarrow looking for a little girl to play family with her."

What was it about Linda this morning, Georgie is thinking. Not a woman who *could* have carried a gun. Or injured a child. Even Oona must have known that about Linda.

"My guess is this," Roosevelt is saying.

"The night before last at the bar at Blake's, Linda saw Oona sitting with your family and she wanted her."

"Does she know who we are?"

"She does."

"Who would have told her? Mr. Blake? I never told him who I was."

"Everyone knows, Georgianna."

"How does she know about my mother's murder?"

"The murder of your mother is a legend. Not just at the camp, but in the town of Missing Lake and in Riverton and all the places inland from the river."

"Sixty-seven years?" Georgie says. "Everyone is dead who was alive then."

"People remember stories."

They are sitting now, their feet side by side resting on the coffee table in front of the unlit fire.

"Nice in here, don't you think?"

"A little cold," Georgie says.

He takes off his jacket and puts it around her shoulders, pulling the soft lining next to her neck.

"The fire's banked and I'll light it unless you're ready for bed."

"Not yet."

"It is almost one a.m."

"I can stay up all night."

Georgie is thinking through the night from midnight to morning.

They'll talk.

Sleepy with the fire and the cold, the smoky room and the smell of pine.

Let's lie down a bit and then we'll go back to the lodge, he'll say to her.

She'll stretch — nonchalant, although that will not be her state of mind. And then, almost casually as though it's a nap they have in mind, they'll go to the camp director's bedroom and lie down on their backs on the double bed side by side. Roosevelt will let his arm fall across her stomach as if by accident. She'll turn, not quite on her side, and lift her head toward his.

"I'm actually not at all tired," Georgie says.

"But I am," Roosevelt says. "Today is a big day in my life and I'm exhausted."

He takes her hand and pulls her up from the couch.

"We're leaving?"

"It's already tomorrow," he says.

They walk down the cabin's steps, the light from his flashlight forming a perfect V on the path ahead, and they step into the light.

"You came here to find out about your father," he says, taking her hand. "I don't have information about the murder beyond what William said."

He leans on his cane for balance.

"But I do have something to tell you about him."

"Is it bad news?" she asks quickly.

"I don't think it will be."

He stops on the path, standing under the stars, his head tilted to the heavens.

"When I moved here, I fell in love with the stars. Many nights alone — and it's cold in the north and often clear — I'd come on the porch of the lodge, which is the only heated building, sit on the steps and look at the stars."

"I love maps of the land," Georgie says, "but I don't really know about the stars."

"There," he says, pointing to the sky. "That brilliant star?"

"I see it," she says.

"It's known as the Pole Star or Polaris or the North Star."

His hand around hers is rough. She's conscious of its strength.

"The Pole Star remains completely still while the other stars move around it."

His cane is under his arm, the beaming flashlight in his hand.

"Or so it seems, but that is deceptive. The stars don't really move of course. It just looks that way because of the rotation of the earth."

"Is that what you were going to tell me?"

He laughs.

"That's not what I am going to tell you," he says catching his breath. "You understand I loved your father."

"Yes." She is tentative. "I do."

"I don't think you are really surprised by what I have told you," he says. "You already knew that answer and were looking for something else."

"What do you mean?"

"You were looking for your father, whom you never really knew," Roosevelt says. "And now you have found him."

They walk to the lodge, along a narrow path that opens to a grassy field high above the river, the air crowded with night sounds: animals, likely skunks, scramble in the bushes, the long hoot of another owl in the distance, the splash of the river against the bank, a light but chilly breeze.

The sky ablaze with stars explodes above them.

"There is a story," Roosevelt says, stopping just before they come to the clearing that leads to the lodge.

"About my father?"

"Yes, about your father."

Lights are on in the main room of the lodge, but upstairs is dark where the rest of the family is sleeping.

They take a seat on the top step under a high sky.

It's cold now, long after midnight, and she moves closer to Roosevelt for the warmth of his body, for his hot breath on her cheeks as they both lean forward against the light wind.

He hesitates as if in search of the right words, but when he speaks, his voice fills the night air.

"When William first came to Washington in the winter of 1930 to live with his Uncle Irving, he got the news that his mother had died in Lithuania."

"I don't know anything about his family except that there was an Uncle Irving," she says.

"His mother was not old but she died, and he was so homesick that he'd sit in the kitchen of Irving's house the way he used to sit in his own kitchen in the village, and watch my mother cook. This I heard from Clem."

"So they were friends."

"They were. He'd go to her house down-town at the end of the day after he finished his job at construction and she'd finished cooking and they'd talk."

"He spoke English?"

"He did speak English, but with an accent which he never lost."

He leans against the post on the side of the porch, Mercy resting her head in his lap.

"And they fell in love."

Georgie is silent.

"They fell in love?"

This is not the story she has imagined.

It would never have crossed her mind that Clementine was more than an excellent cook who worked at the house where her father lived when he arrived in America.

"They were lovers? Your mother told you that?"

"She did," he says. "And then after a couple of years he moved to Michigan to study, and that's where he met your mother, as you know."

She sits in silence beside him.

"No wonder you wanted to be in touch with me."

"We have a common history and I was the only one who knew," he says. "It was a loss."

"But tell me . . ." Georgie says under her

breath. "I don't quite understand why William didn't take Clem with him when he moved to Michigan?"

He leans forward, rests his elbows on his knees.

"Because it was 1933 in segregated Washington, D.C. That would not have been possible."

Georgie stares out at the starlit darkness. Her breath thin, her heart thumping in her chest. Even Roosevelt must be able to hear it.

All along, she had expected to discover simple news to close the book on William Grove. Yes or no. He did it or he did not. She was prepared for the worst.

But not for this news.

Roosevelt stretches his legs down the steps, crossing them at the ankles.

"Now you understand, Georgianna," he says. "This is the only real answer I have to the question you came here to ask me."

"I don't know what to say," she says.

"Nothing to say," Roosevelt replies.

"Except . . ." Her voice so soft he needs to lean down close to her lips to hear. "Since that is what happened between them, maybe we have an obligation."

He wraps his arm around her shivering

shoulders, leaning his head against the top step.

"See above us, on a clear night like this, there is a blanket of stars," he says.

"It's a beautiful night."

"I've studied the galaxy at the library in Riverton and think of myself as a kind of celestial navigator," he says. "Often when I'm alone at camp, I sit here at night if it's clear and the sky is full of stars."

He lays his hand gently on her knee.

"It's a funny thing, but knowing something about the stars gives me a sense of power not *over* anything — more like believing in God, which I do not. But that kind of power."

"What am I looking at?" Georgie asks.

"You're looking at the W lying on its side facing north. See it? And Cassiopeia. A very bright star named for an ancient queen."

"I think I see it," she says, her voice thin as paper.

It is as if her lungs have closed down and all she wants to hear is Roosevelt talking to her. Just words tumbling out in *his* voice. About anything — stars or trees or birds. Even words in another language.

"Just talk to me," she says.

"I will," he says.

And he does.

The familiar pressure on Georgie's chest seems to be lifting. She can actually feel it deflating, disappearing. So accustomed was she to its presence, she had not even known it was there.

Now in its place, a feeling of lightness.

"I need to know the galaxy," she says.

"I'll tell you what I see," he says. "Above Cassiopeia is her husband Cepheus with a pointed hat and a pigtail. And then to the left, the Giraffe, but you can't really see him."

"It's harder to see the shapes than it is on a land map," she says.

"True. But what I like about the stars is that you can count on them night after night. Every star in the sky rises and sets about four minutes earlier each day than it did the day before. And every new year we are back exactly where we started," he says. "That order matters to me."

"Just name them for me. I love names," she says. "Like Roosevelt."

He laughs.

"There's Andromeda," he says, "and the Whale and Perseus and Pegasus."

Georgie is lulled into a kind of calm listening to him. She leans back and rests her head on his chest.

"Is that all the news for me tonight?"

"It's all I have," Roosevelt says. "Coming on eighty, I asked myself what if you *never* found out about your father and my mother? What then?"

"Then I would never know."

She closes her eyes and stretches her arm across her forehead to cut out the light of the dazzling sky and shelter her eyes wet with tears.

"Tell me everything you know about the sky tonight," Georgie says without lifting her arm. "And what is happening up there. What everybody is doing."

"Everybody?"

"The stars," she says.

And he does.

The story of every star visible on this clear and remarkable night.

Maybe Georgie falls asleep. She is aware of sinking into the wooden steps, aware that her mind is empty, her body slipping away, and she wonders in an abstract kind of way what is happening to her that feels at once like dying and living, as if she will awaken from this slow disappearance to herself.

An image wanders across her mind and she catches hold before it slips away.

She is in a large room, a black night outside the window, sitting on a couch with her father, probably in Chicago, and maybe she is already four. Maybe younger.

"We had to make a picture of our home today at nursery school," she tells him. "And I told the teacher we live in an apartment. Not a home. And she asked me 'Isn't an apartment also home?' And I didn't know the answer."

"Home is you, Georgie," her father said. "You take it wherever you go."

Had that happened? she wonders now. Or did she imagine or hope it was what he had said. Or did it matter at all whether it was real or imagined? Finally, they were the same thing.

Georgie leans over and touches Roosevelt's face, lays her cold hand on top of his, bristly and warm against her palm.

"Roosevelt?" she begins.

But there are no words.

Above them, the clear, cold night sky is ablaze with stars as if the stars themselves are falling out of heaven, scattering light across the earth.

FROM THE MEMOIR OF THOMAS DAVIES
(FOR PUBLICATION)

I am sitting in the lodge of Camp Minnie HaHa (latitude/ longitude TK) located on the Bone River, sitting on the floor in a corner of the room watching my family drink champagne out of paper cups. It is six in the morning. They are gathered at the end of the long table laughing and crying and hugging each other.

Roosevelt — whom I had expected to be either the hero or the villain of this story — is serving spinach omelets and waffles and blueberry muffins.

Nicolas, my disagreeable uncle, is honest-to-God singing.

Beside me, my cousin Oona, sensing that in this room I am the only sensible human (she says *who-man*), lies on my legs.

I simply do not understand adults.

We came on this journey, which has had its problems, to discover whether my great-grandfather William Grove murdered his wife at the Missing Lake campsite in 1941. Or not.

The answer as it has turned out is *Roosevelt*.

The news is that he isn't the villain some of us were imagining him to be. Rather his mother, Clementine, the camp's cook who never got to cook, was my great-grandfather's girlfriend. Or *lover,* as Venus told me — whatever that means.

Now the question of *who* killed Georgie's mother is no longer of any interest to the adults.

It is however still important to me.

I cannot imagine that the students at Alice Deal Junior High School off Nebraska Avenue in Washington, D.C., will have an interest in the story of my great-grandfather's *lover* as a satisfactory replacement story for murder.

Therefore it falls to me to write the story of the murder as I imagine it might have happened.

These are the significant facts of the night of June 17, 1941, as far as I know.

1. William Grove's village in Lithuania is about to be invaded by the Nazis. The chances are good that William's father will be shot or sent to

the gas chambers to die.

2. William had a love affair with Clementine — (*passionate love affair* was Georgie's description this morning after a glass of champagne).

3. Josephine, William's wife, does not like William because he is a Jew. The explanation Georgie gave us this morning had to do with anti-Semitism and the War and Josephine's depression and Clementine coming on the trip with Roosevelt and nobody knowing the real identity of Clementine as girlfriend of my great-grandfather. Including Roosevelt.

4. There has been no mention today of the *murder.* That is the kind of craziness adults seem to enjoy.

5. So this trip we have taken to Missing Lake was to discover one thing. And now we arrive to discover another that seems to the adults even better than finding the answer to the first thing.

6. So you see my dilemma.

THE STORY OF THE
MURDER OF JOSEPHINE GROVE
AS I IMAGINE IT

It is the middle of the night. William and Josephine are still awake, maybe lying in their tent, maybe talking, probably fighting — but they are not visible to the rest of the camp should people happen to be awake.

Georgianna Grove who is four years old is sleeping in the tent with the camp nurse far away from her parents and close to the water.

Josephine is in a vicious humor because William is in love with Clementine, who is beautiful and strong. Contrary to Josephine, who is overweight and unhappy.

I should mention that next to William's sleeping bag is a rope used to anchor the canoes.

William is lying in his sleeping bag on his back, his arm like a pillow under his head. He is thinking about his father standing in the street in his village in front of his house in a line with other neighbors waiting to be assassinated.

I have seen photographs of Jews lined up,

their backs to the firing squad, their arms over their heads in brave surrender.

Josephine is lying in her sleeping bag, her hands folded on her stomach, and she is thinking about the beautiful Clementine kissing William on the lips, the way I used to watch my father kiss my mother after they danced in the dining room in Chicago.

"William," she says, interrupting his misery. "You are a disgusting man."

William keeps his eyes tight shut and does not respond.

"I wish you were dead," she says. "I want to be the one to shoot you in the head and watch as your brain splashes out all over the sleeping bag."

William opens his eyes just in case she suddenly has access to a rifle.

"You smell of skunk," she says.

William sits up in his sleeping bag ready to spring in case she attacks.

"I want to shoot Clementine McCrary and watch her bleed though her shirt, writhing in agony on the ground."

That is what Josephine says.

William's hands are in a fist, his body tight-wired for action.

"Jew," she says.

William leaps up and without thinking, he grabs the thick rope beside his sleeping bag, wraps it around Josephine's neck and holds it tight until she is dead.

He is tired, but he cannot get any sleep with his dead wife lying next to him, so he picks her up and carries her to the edge of the forest, where he drops her in the root bed of a pine tree. She is discovered the following morning by James Willow, the head counselor.

Walking back to his tent in the middle of the dark night, he is not sorry about Josephine. He knows that he will admit to killing her because he is an honorable man. He imagines that in Lithuania, his father, Dr. Geringas, has been assassinated.

What breaks his heart is Georgianna. His daughter. His only child.

This is the story I imagine to have happened at Missing Lake, June 17, 1941.

It is the story I will tell when I go back to Alice Deal Junior High in September.

Georgie will *not* be upset that I tell this story.

She believes the imagination is the truth.

Before we leave Camp Minnie HaHa, I plan to give this journal to Roosevelt McCrary. I'll ask him to bury it at the campsite at Missing Lake. He'll need to bury it deep so the archeologists digging hundreds, maybe thousands of years from now (probably a huge city will have developed on the banks of the Bone River), will discover the journal and put it in a glass case at the Smithsonian Museum of American History in Washington, D.C., with a sign under the glass which reads:

The Journal of Thomas Davies,
grandson of Georgianna Grove,
in the year 2008 A.D.

ACKNOWLEDGMENTS

To my first agent, then husband, Timothy Seldes, always true to his word, who stayed as long as he possibly could.

To my family, to whom I am always grateful but never more than with this novel — to my life coaches: *the kids:* Theo, Noah, Isaak, Henry, Julian, Padget, Eliza, Aden, Elodie, and Isla.

To my agent, Gail Hochman; my editor, Jill Bialosky; her assistant, Drew Weitman; and all the team at W. W. Norton.

I am grateful to Yaddo for time to work, two visits during the writing of this novel. To George Mason University and the many Mason students who have enriched my life.

ABOUT THE AUTHOR

Susan Richards Shreve is the author of fifteen novels, a memoir, and thirty books for children. She has received a Guggenheim Fellowship and a National Endowment grant, among other honors. A professor of creative writing at George Mason University and former chairman of the PEN/Faulkner Foundation, Shreve lives in Washington, D.C.

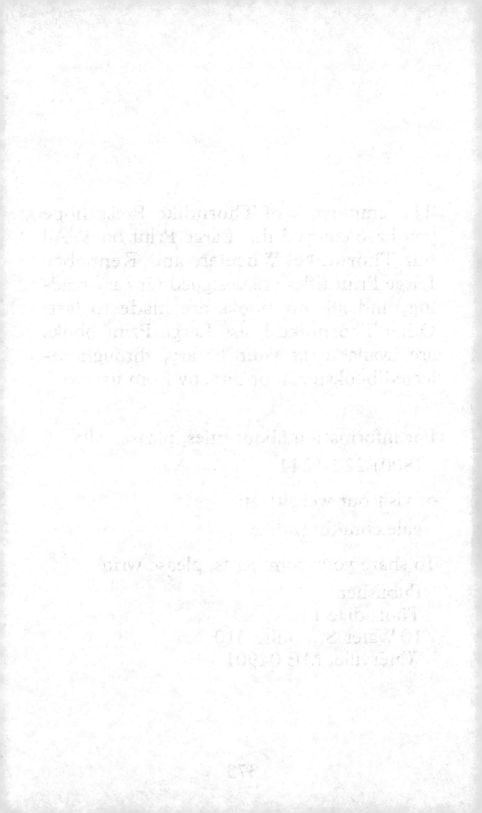